A Slice of Life

Life Stories

Thom Gossom, Jr.

Best Gurl inc.

Fort Walton Beach, FL

A Slice of Life

Editor: Randall Horton
Cover art: David Paladino
Author photo: Anna Ritch Photography

ISBN 978-0-9890865-4-7
LCCN 2015952691

Best Gurl inc.
PO Box 4235
Fort Walton Beach, FL 32549

Printed in the United States of America

To joyce and Mom G, the Best Gurls

Contents

Introduction

You eat the pie one slice at a time. That's been my philosophy with the *Slice of Life* collection.

When I began, I wondered where the characters would lead me. I had stories to tell. Many had simmered for way too long.

Are they true stories? No. They're life stories.

In *A Slice of Life, Another Slice of Life,* and *The Rest of the Pie,* average people face their own extraordinary circumstances, their own veritable moment of truth. They stand at the proverbial fork in the road faced with choices, whether their own or life's dictates.

A Slice of Life mirrors the first season of life, reflected in a newly integrated Alabama of the 1960s and 70s.

Another Slice of Life moves through the decadence of the 1980s.

The Rest of the Pie reflects life's journey in the 1990s and 21st century.

The stories in this book are fiction. In the telling, some names of public figures are used. However, any facts, incidents, and characters that may resemble real life are purely coincidental.

My job was to use my imagination to make the most of the raw material found in life, and that is what I have done.

Thom Gossom, Jr.

The man who has no imagination has no wings.
—Muhammad Ali

The Crimson Tide

It was game day! Game day, baby! Trey was ready! He'd been for his morning jog. He had on his new red sweatshirt. His chest sufficiently stuck out; the intensity simmered inside him rising to a game day boil. It was November. The air was crisp, not yet cold; the leaves were colorful, and The University of Alabama, The Crimson Tide, was playing LSU this evening in Baton Rouge, Louisiana.

Jesus, Mary, and Joseph!

Passing riders in red vehicles hollered "ROLL TIDE!" at him out of their windows. Trey waved back, not yet ready to vocally express his jubilation.

He swung his shiny unused rake into the sea of red and yellow leaves blanketing his yard. Truck, the black fellow who had done the yard for his father the past ten years, had come on Tuesday with his crew. They hauled off fifty giant bags of leaves. Thursday's wind gusts undid all their work.

Trey diligently raked the gazebo area. They would gather here after the game.

He checked his watch. Five hours until game time. He still had to make a run to the liquor store, the butcher, and the deli. Back at home, he'd fire up the grill for steaks, fish, and chicken. By kickoff, he would be in his chair, food on his tray, drink in hand, and remote at his command, just like his dad.

The first Alabama game in the new, old house would be a family affair.

Donna, Trey's college girlfriend and wife of twenty years and Tiffany, their teenaged daughter, were out "spending money." They would come home with the latest fashion, Alabama red of course, to watch the evening's game on television.

The extended family would be here—"Hodge the Hippie," Hodge's wife, Mary, and their family of dogs: labs Sam and Sally, and Roscoe, their "ghetto dog from the projects."

Hodge would bring some good bud. Samson, he called it.

The closer it got to game time, the more Trey thought of Big Willis and the Alabama game days of his youth. Big Willis loved game day. On game day, Trey's dad, Big Willis, was transformed into a laughing, drinking, overweight, story-telling bundle of fun.

"This is family," Big Willis would loudly proclaim, his booming voice echoing throughout the house.

Like his dad, Trey declared the LSU game Family Day. It would be an all-day party of preparation, anticipation, game-talk buzz, and sips of Jim Beam culminating with Trey reprising his dad's game day rituals—having friends over, grilling, and watching the game with liquor flowing.

. . .

As a boy, Trey had been inseparable from Big Willis. If Big Willis was at the golf course, so was Trey. The barbershop. They got their hair cut at the same time in separate chairs. Big Willis and Little Willis they were called, until Trey's mom, Betty Lou, stepped in and insisted her son be called Trey. She told her son, "When you're grown you're not going to like being referred to as 'little' anything. The girls sure won't like it." Big Willis didn't agree but rolled with it as long as he had Trey and Alabama Football.

Big Willis lived and breathed Crimson Tide football. He made sure his only child and son, Trey, got a heavy dose. They went to every game, home and away. Betty Lou didn't attend the away games, so it was "just us boys this weekend," Big Willis would declare. With no Betty Lou around, Big Willis would splurge on whatever Trey wanted and would introduce his son as Little Willis to anyone who would listen.

The first game Trey could remember was Alabama vs. the University of California in the mid-1960s. What a night in Birmingham's Legion Field! The stadium's lights lit up the night sky in the western end of town. Excitement crackled like electricity. Alabama's Million Dollar Band revved up the crowd dressed in a sea of red. Cheers of "Roll Tide!" reverberated throughout the stadium.

Bear Bryant, the legendary Alabama Coach, strolled casually out of the locker room, his houndstooth hat sinking low on his head. He wore a wrinkled off-white shirt and inexpensive slacks, carried a rolled-up program in his hand and nonchalantly leaned against the goal post. The Bear was in his lair.

Trey, wide-eyed and mystified, hungrily took it all in.

After Alabama had beaten "the smart boys from Berkley" 66-0, Big Willis took Trey down onto the field and let him run across the beautiful nighttime green grass. Trey ran wildly in no specific direction. He even approached an Alabama football player he later discovered was the great All-American linebacker, Leroy Jordan. Leroy gave Trey one of his sweatbands. Trey ran as close as he could to Coach Bryant, as he was being hustled off the field by his personal guardians, two Alabama State Troopers. Trey had met the legendary Coach before with his dad. He wanted to see if Coach would recognize him. Bear didn't. He seemed to be in a daze and just wanted to get off the field. Trey continued running aimlessly, with no intention and no direction, until he ran up on Big Willis. He jumped into Big Willis' arms, giving him the sweatband bounty he had scored earlier from the Alabama linebacker. Big Willis' hug gave Trey a comfort and security that all boys want from their fathers.

Trey and Big Willis walked off the field together, hand-in-hand. It was the happiest night of Trey's life.

. . .

Big Willis, Willis Edward Williams, Jr., was one of Birmingham, Alabama's self-proclaimed elite. He was educated at the University of Alabama, where the football team won championships with regularity. Those championships, for some, outshone the darker spotlight of the city's 1960s civil rights wars, and rankings of 49th out of the fifty states in education and health. The outside agitators, with their "singing and civil rights," didn't allow the proper spotlight to shine on Alabama football. Still, Coach Bear Bryant was civic pride. Little boys in Alabama grew up wanting to play quarterback for the Crimson Tide.

Big Willis, the Executive Vice President of the First American Bank, was responsible for, among other things, the bank's advertising. Early in his career, he hit it off with Coach Bryant over a drink of red whiskey and a card game and scored a major coup when the bank agreed to sponsor the coach's show, signing the great coach to a twenty-year contract to do the bank's commercials. Coach and Big Willis became business associates and drinking buddies. When asked by the local newspaper why a twenty-year contract, Big Willis answered, "Because bank policy wouldn't allow me to sign him for life."

A southern, larger-than-life caricature, Big Willis was beloved at First American. He made loans to his employees that helped them buy houses, cars, and send their children to college. He financed pickups for Henry, the black fellow who did his lawn until he couldn't work anymore and turned it over to his son, Truck, whom Big Willis also financed.

A big man with big appetites, Big Willis dominated every second of every day. When he wasn't drinking, there was not a better fellow in the world. When he was drinking, which he did daily, he could be crass and arrogant and could suck all the air out of a room. Most nights Big Willis spent alone in his study. The day's business done and family obligations honored, Big Willis would retreat to his study and his personal library of Alabama game films from the week's taping and coach's show. Proud of his collection of over 100 games of Alabama football, Big Willis had his film library catalogued and he would put on a show of Alabama's biggest victories at the many parties he and Betty Lou threw.
As Trey grew, so did Big Willis' demands.

Big Willis had played ball in high school, a linebacker. In one legendary game, he'd gotten three teeth knocked out playing against "some rednecks from down 'round Git Back Alabama." Big Willis retrieved his bloody teeth from the grass, handed them to the referee, blood and all, and ran back into his team's huddle with a mouth full of blood grinning like a madman. On the next play, he violently stuffed the other team's running back in the hole and let out a raging, blood curdling scream, his own blood flying everywhere. Big Willis was a tough son-of-a-bitch.

He had it all planned out for Trey. Trey would play junior high and high school ball and if Big Willis got lucky and Trey was worth a shit, Big Willis would negotiate him a one-year tryout at Alabama. Next, there would be Alabama Law School and one day, President of First American. Wouldn't that be something to talk about?

But a detour happened on the way to the family dynasty. As Trey grew older, Big Willis became easily disappointed in Trey. At the top of that list, Big Willis wanted Trey to play football. Trey didn't want to. Trey liked the game, but he had never needed or wanted to play. Big Willis needed him to. Trey refused. "Just give it a try," Big Willis encouraged. Trey declined.

Big Willis cut Trey's allowance. "Just try out," he begged. "You'll be proud you did one day. One day you can say you played at the University of Alabama under Coach Bear Bryant. Boy, that's worth its weight in gold in this town."

Instead, Trey joined some of his friends in running cross-country track. He liked the solitude of it. There was "an individual freedom to running," he tried to explain to Big Willis. The track choice infuriated Big Willis. "Faggot ass track," he snarled. Big Willis refused to go to any track meets.

Trey rebelled. He began passing on his parents' social invitations. At fifteen, he let his hair grow down his back and started a band called The Long Hairs. After the band's gigs, he would hang out at a hippie bar for teens with blacks and anti-war protestors in "unsafe" downtown Birmingham.

Big Willis didn't give up. On Trey's sixteenth birthday, Big Willis bought Trey a brand new shiny red Camaro convertible. It was beautiful. Trey drove around his hippie and black friends for a while and then traded it for a Volkswagen van for The Long Hairs.

Big Willis' toleration for Trey's disrespect slowly wore at him. If Big Willis said left, Trey went right. If Big Willis got pissed at the "niggers" for demonstrating in downtown Birmingham, Trey would lecture his dad about how the Afro-Americans had been mistreated. They drifted in opposite directions. Trey still went to the Alabama games, but he enjoyed them less and less.

At seventeen, the Crimson Tide split father and son for good.

Trey, feeling his impending manhood and the need to rebel, announced he had gone to his last Alabama game with Big Willis. "I'm done with football," he told Big Willis. "Not going anymore. Want to pursue my music and running track." Trey even refused to watch the games on television with Big Willis.

Out of frustration, Big Willis drove a lifelong wedge between him and his son.

It was the annual state rivalry, the Alabama–Auburn game. Big Willis demanded that Trey go with the family. The event would be a huge social affair with Big Willis entertaining well-to-do bank clients and their families. Trey, now thin and lean, his hair snaking down his back, arrogantly refused. "You can't make me."

The tension in the house between father and son rose to a boiler pitch.

Betty Lou didn't have the stomach for fighting. She withdrew and did what she always did: she took one of her pills. Where Big Willis was loud and abrasive, she was quiet, and most of the time under the influence of one of the many pills she took.

At one time, Betty Lou had been a dreamer, quiet and dignified, a looker, a country girl, a good student with potential. She had dreamed of practicing law with indigent clients, "giving back to society." She met Big Willis in law school and the rest was their history.

In a whirlwind courtship, Big Willis hounded her until she said yes and left her own dreams behind. Now, the years of Big Willis' domination and pills had backed her down to nothing more than a lapdog. It was how she coped.

She stood up to Big Willis on one occasion. "If you don't stop drinking," she warned him, "I'm not having any more children." He didn't, and she didn't.

Betty Lou sank into the life of a pill head.

Dressed and ready for the big event, Big Willis grabbed Trey by the arm and snatched him up into midair from the couch. "Dammit! Stop being an asshole, get your suit on, and let's go! It's a big game!" Trey slapped Big Willis' arm from his own, breaking Big Willis' grip. "I've got a gig downtown with my band," he spat. Big Willis, the smell of Jim Beam oozing from his pores, grabbed Trey again and would not let go. "I said get your shit on!"

Trey was taken aback. Big Willis was loud, unruly, and drunk, but he had never been physical with Betty Lou or Trey.

Betty Lou stood across the room, her eyes glazed over. She would not interfere.

Trey tried to jerk away from Big Willis. Big Willis, leveraging his bulk, squeezed Trey in a bear hug. Trey twisted, pushing Big Willis away from him. Big Willis, out of shape and breathing heavily, tumbled off balance and fell heavily onto the sofa.

Uh-oh shot through Trey's brain.

Big Willis' eyes flashed red-hot anger. He was tired of the bullshit. His frustration flowed. The whiskey boiled his blood. He crossed the line!

Big Willis' right hand shot across Trey's face with a force like a thunderclap that sent Trey's light frame flying across the floor. Big Willis rushed in, hunkered down over his son, his fist tightly balled, his breaths heaving up and down. His round belly pushed against his pin-striped vest and suspenders. He dared his son to get up. "Git your sorry ass up!" He spit out the words, saliva flying from his mouth. "Git up!"

Trey got up, angry, ready to fight the first fight of his life. Big Willis swung again at Trey. Trey raised his hands in self-defense. Big Willis took Trey's defense as offense and went on an all-out attack.

Big Willis lit into Trey, knocking him down. "You pussy!" Big Willis screamed. His rage flowed. He slapped Trey again across the face. Again. Again. Tears flowed uncontrollably from Big Willis' eyes. Each slap was for years of impudence and Trey's embarrassing refusal to play football.

Trey didn't fight back. He didn't defend himself. He took Big Willis' best blows; his dead eyes locked onto Big Willis' fiery ones and seemed to say to his dad, *You can't hurt me*. It was a look Big Willis would never be able to erase from his brain.

Betty Lou took a deep breath. Her eyes rolled up into her head. She fainted, her glass of scotch falling before her to the floor. She fell onto the beautiful hardwood floor flush on her face and onto the glass, cutting herself deeply on her jaw, creating a scar she would wear through three plastic surgeries. Betty Lou rolled over bleeding and passed out.

Big Willis rushed to revive his wife. He shook her, poured water on her, and gave her a drink to bring her around. "You okay, baby doll?" he cooed. He poured a drink of scotch down her throat. He searched for her pills and forced one down.

"Call emergency!" Trey shouted. Big Willis refused. It would be embarrassing. After all, he was Big Willis, somebody. "You okay?" he asked her again. She came around. She asked for a pill and Big Willis gave her another one. He carried her to her bedroom.

Trey fled to his room, locked the door, and did not come out for a week. His mom reported him sick to the school principal. She had Beulah, the black cook and housekeeper, who was Truck's mom, leave food outside his door.

Trey never attended another Alabama game with Big Willis. He never watched another Alabama game with Big Willis.

This lasted until Big Willis died.

. . .

Trey got the last laugh. He took seven years to graduate college. His dad's money paid the bills and his influence kept Trey out of Vietnam. When graduation day finally rolled around, Big Willis ridiculed Trey.

"What did they do? Let you out for good behavior?" he asked. Trey's grade point average of .88 ensured he would not be following Big Willis' dreams of law school and becoming the bank's president.

Trey further alienated Big Willis. He refused to join his dad's fraternity, or any fraternity. He passed on all the sorority dates he was set up with. He passed on the football tickets in his family's priority seating section. He had it all: money, prestige, and connections, but he refused to play along. He did it all to spite Big Willis.

Trey was determined that he would run his own life, not Big Willis.

Trey, now a hippie with hair flowing down his back, dressed

in well-worn jeans, Chuck Taylor Converse basketball shoes, and army jackets, became active in liberal political causes. He marched on Washington D.C. against the war and made the national news when he was randomly interviewed by ABC News.

The gulf between the two men grew into a gorge and then a canyon until Trey struck out for what Big Willis called "the land of fruits and nuts"—California.

Trey and Donna, his college girlfriend, sold his van and hitchhiked across the country. They landed jobs in Los Angeles. Trey worked as a late night manager in a sleazy Hollywood coffee shop where he met many of the young prostitutes who'd been sidetracked on their way to becoming movie starlets. He met up-and-coming musicians in the Hollywood music scene. Donna found a job as an assistant to a young hotshot movie producer, to whom she gave a couple of blow jobs, but never told her husband.

Trey started a band with four other southern trust fund babies, The Lost Boys. The band made two albums and had one hit, "You Don't Know," making enough money to get them out of the LA grit and grime. They moved north to Santa Cruz. Trey and Donna opened a coffee shop, bought a cabin in the woods next to a creek, and decided to start a family. Tiffany was born and for ten years, things were great. Then, everyone married and had children. The guys were no longer in demand as a band, and with royalties declining, money was running out. Trey reached out to an old hippie buddy from college, Hodge, who had never had a social security number. Hodge operated out of the state of Alabama, selling marijuana to dealers.

. . .

Trey and Hodge met as freshmen at the University of Alabama. Trey, attracted to Hodge's outside-the-system lifestyle, moved into Hodge's trailer. Trey had never lived in a house on wheels and Hodge had never lived in one without. Hodge trafficked in good bud, selling it to rich kids on campus. According to Big Willis, Hodge had that ground-in dirt, long stringy blonde hair, and poor cracker look. "PWT," is what Big Willis called Hodge—"Poor white trash."

Hodge remained in Alabama when Trey struck out for the West Coast.

When the call from his old friend came, Hodge hooked Trey up with a West Coast Latin operative named Hector, "The Big Enchilada." Before the cartels took over, Hector and his homies imported half of the marijuana into the United States. Hector, a big fan of The Lost Boys, was excited to meet Trey.

They struck a deal. Trey cut his hair and became the perfect mule—white, respectable looking, and non-threatening.

The typical routine for Trey was like going to the office, albeit the office was an entire country. Trey would fly to San Diego, check into a motel, check out the next morning and commandeer the truck or van he found in the space where his rental car had been. He then drove to New Jersey, checked into a motel, checked out the next morning, and left with a car in place of the truck. In the trunk of the car would be a suitcase Trey delivered to The Big Enchilada. Once, on a run to Miami, Trey, dog-tired, checked into a motel in Mississippi. He opened the suitcase. A million dollars stared back at him. He slammed it shut and locked it. He hardly slept, hugging the suitcase close throughout the night. He never opened another.

Trey was paid $10,000-$25,000 per trip in cash. He made at least one or two trips a month.

In all that time, there was one close call and once he nearly froze to death.

Driving across Kansas in sub-freezing temperatures, he'd gotten a truck with no heat. He nearly lost his toes to the cold. He pulled into a motel when he couldn't stand the ache in his feet anymore. When he complained, Hector suggested that he buy a pair of thick socks.

Another time, he'd been pulled over in New Jersey on the turnpike. The van's left taillight was not working. The trooper, with "good ole boy" written all over him, approached the van ready for danger. He wore reflector shades and a tight-fitting state patrol uniform. He flipped the switch on his holster. Trey's life hung in the balance. He was driving a van full of marijuana in New Jersey with no other apparent business reason to be in the state. He imagined himself in jail. He imagined having to call Donna but even worse having to call Betty Lou and have her tell Big Willis. Trey sunk to his lowest depth. *Oh, my God*, he thought.

The suspicious cop asked for Trey's license. He looked the van up and down. His look scoured the passenger seat of the van, the ashtray. He walked to the back of the van. Trey's heart jumped.

"You mind stepping out of the van?" the cop asked.

Trey stepped out.

The cop looked Trey up and down. Trey tried not to fidget.

Cars whisked by. The cop stood deathly still, his hand at the ready…and then…a grin creased his face.

"Roll Tide," the cop volunteered.

"Whaa…" Trey started to say.

"Did you go to Alabama?" the cop asked.

Trey was wearing a University of Alabama T-shirt. An *Oh shit!* feeling of relief rushed through his brain.

"I went to Alabama," the cop went on. "Had some relatives down south. Tried out for the football team. Had to get back closer to home though."

Trey scrambled for words.

The cop handed Trey his license and took his shades off. "So, do you get to many games?"

. . .

After three years, Trey had enough money to make his move back to Alabama. But he would not go back to Birmingham. He still had not reached out to Big Willis, nor had Big Willis to him.

He and Donna moved two hundred and fifty miles south of Birmingham to Alabama's Orange Beach and opened a small coffee shop. They lived the life of laid back, modest, small business owners on the beach. Betty Lou would visit when she and Big Willis vacationed at their beach condo one hundred miles due east in Destin, Florida. Betty Lou, Tiffany, and Donna occasionally would do a shopping excursion, and Tiffany would visit her grandparents. But Big Willis never visited. Neither did Trey. They spoke exactly three times over the years, two Christmases and on Big Willis' seventy-fifth birthday. Neither man would make the first move for a face-to-face visit. "Fuck him," Big Willis would drunkenly grunt.

Trey refused to discuss it.

When the old man died, Trey attended the funeral. He felt awkward, empty, lost. He didn't cry, but he'd lost something. At the funeral, he saw so many of the people he had known growing up in Birmingham. It made him feel good, nostalgic. It made him see Big Willis differently. Big Willis had been a clown, a drunk, and abusive, but several thousand people turned out to give him love at his funeral. There was genuine respect for Big Willis.

Betty Lou slipped into a deep depression when Big Willis died. She died six months later from an accidental overdose.

Reluctantly, Trey moved his family from the beach to his parents' home in the upscale Birmingham community of Mountain Brook. Although sad to leave the beach, Trey and his family would now have more money than they would ever need. They made the move.

In California, Trey never watched, attended, or read about an Alabama football game. It was too painful. After the family moved to Orange Beach, Trey sat down alone one Saturday and watched a game. It had been three decades. He slowly progressed to watching a game with Donna and then with Tiffany and Donna as a family.

This would be his first Alabama game in the house since he was a boy.

. . .

Game time grew closer. Unconsciously, Trey followed Big Willis' routines for game day. It was funny how it was all coming back to him. It was strange to be back in the house he'd grown up in after all these years. It was stranger still to be getting ready for an Alabama game, here. He and Donna had not gotten around to changing much. The furniture was still the same. Big Willis and Betty Lou's art still hung from the walls. Memories, both good and bad, were plentiful.

Trey refused to go into Big Willis' study. Nobody did. It was sacred.

Passing a hallway mirror, Trey caught a glimpse of himself. The thought and image flashed across his brain. No longer reed-thin, Trey had filled out, grown a gut. He was out of shape. He'd cut his hair. The thought rested on his brain. He looked like Big Willis.

Trey ran his pre-game errands picking up the liquor and food for the evening. He was energized. He had not felt emotion over a college football game since he was a kid. College football dominated life in Birmingham. There was constant media chatter and talk at the office water coolers, hot dog stands, barber shops, and Sundays after church. "Roll Tide," a customer in the butcher market greeted Trey. "Roll Tide," Trey returned, a little unsure of himself. Like Big Willis before him, Trey selected the finest grades of meat. His cell chirped. It was Hodge. He'd put $500 on Alabama.

Trey cooked chicken, fish, and steak just like Big Willis would have. It was delicious. Hodge brought along some tequila and monster bud.

With Jim Beam flowing like water, Trey morphed into someone Tiffany and Donna did not recognize. Trey became Big Willis.

He led the "Roll Tide" opening cheer, letting the letter "L" in the word "Roll" linger across his tongue before ending the cheer, "Tide, Roll," just like Big Willis had done so many times. He showed Tiffany how to balance on the couch and holler "Ro-l-l-l-l Tide!" just like Big Willis had taught him.

Alabama jumped on LSU and never looked back. The Tide steamrolled the Tigers from the Bayou. Trey was the entertainment. He argued with the refs, and barked with the dogs, Sam, Sally, and Roscoe. After the game, Trey taught everyone the Victory Walk, just like Big Willis had taught him. He stuck out his chest, raised his chin, and high-stepped like a rooster. Everyone laughed, even Hodge who was so stoned he'd slept through the second half. The family all got to their feet and victory walked around the family room.

Underneath the booze and the weed, Trey questioned himself. Why was he behaving like Big Willis? Why? He didn't want to be like Big Willis.

Big Willis was still sucking all the air out of the room.

The others moved out to the gazebo. They didn't know it, but that was also a Big Willis move. Big Willis would hold court under the gazebo. *Leave me alone*, Trey thought, shoving aside the thoughts of Big Willis. He rejoined the group.

They smoked a big bud, all except Tiffany. It was Trey's rule. She had to wait until she was twenty-one. Tiffany didn't mind. She wasn't into the stuff. She enjoyed athletics and played on the high school basketball team.

Trey downed another drink. His voice rose louder and louder. He dominated the conversation.

Tiffany had never seen her dad like this. She'd seen him drink, but he never behaved in this dominating, aggressive manner.

Tiffany said good night.

Donna, reading her daughter's mood, held on to Tiffany's goodnight hug longer than usual. Like Betty Lou before her, Donna let her husband's needs come first. It was the only way Trey could cope, and she knew it. She loved her husband but wished better for her daughter.

The foursome talked and drank, smoked, and talked some more. They caught up on the good old days. Trey, still catching up to college football, marveled that the game had changed from white athletes to almost all black ones. He wondered aloud what Big Willis would have thought of that. "All that matters is the jersey, man," Hodge explained.

The night ended with everyone happily exhausted. Hodge, Mary, Sam, Sally, and Roscoe would stay in the guesthouse out back. Trey and Donna drunkenly hung on to each other and made their way to the bedroom.

Trey's first Alabama game in his parents' house since childhood had been a good one. It was the best time Trey could remember in a long, long time.

. . .

Trey and Donna made wild exciting love that night in his parents' bed. It had been a while for them. Trey was drunk and sloppy and Donna was hungry for him. They grunted and groaned until they spent themselves. Trey held on uncharacteristically tight.

Donna fell asleep lying on Trey's arm. Trey dozed, but then lay awake, unable to sleep.

Trey eased his arm from under Donna's head. He slipped on his pajamas and walked to Big Willis' study. Trey had not been in

Big Willis' study since he was a child when he and Big Willis would watch game films together. He thought about it. He went in. The wood paneled room looked the same as it had so many years before. Trey moved to Big Willis' favorite chair and sat. There were pictures of Trey as a child and teen, pictures of the family and many pictures of Trey and Big Willis, father and son, grinning at an Alabama game. Surprisingly, there was a picture of Trey and his family at their beach home. It was the only picture of Trey after his sixteenth birthday. Trey wondered how it got there.

Trey read through the titles of his dad's library of Alabama games, Alabama vs. Auburn, Alabama vs. Tennessee, Alabama vs. Florida and many more, all in sequential order. There were gaps, games missing. Trey reasoned these were the games that Alabama lost, the memories too painful to relive through film. A package labeled in red sat amongst the game tapes. Trey and Leroy Jordan: "PRIVATE—FOR TREY'S 21ST BIRTHDAY."

Trey opened the package. The old sweatbands he had gotten that night, another lifetime ago, were there. They smelled, but that was not the point. There was also an aged videotape.

Tape in the machine, Trey settled in Big Willis' chair and hit *Play* on the remote. The old black and white footage ran in vertical and horizontal lines making it impossible to tell what was on the screen.

The lines cleared enough to see.

It's the end of a game and little Trey is running across the field, running up to Leroy Jordan and getting his sweatbands. The tape continues to run. On the tape, Little Trey runs until he sees Big Willis. Trey jumps up and hugs Big Willis who picks him up and swings him around in the air. Trey hands Big Willis the sweatbands. Trey and Big Willis walk off the field together, hand-in-hand.

Trey had never seen this footage before but he remembered the night as the best time he had ever had with Big Willis. He remembered Big Willis letting him run on the field. He now knew Big Willis had arranged this taping especially for him, as a gift for his twenty-first birthday. Being in charge of the coach's show, it would have been no problem to get the cameraman to shoot Trey as he ran onto the field. Trey remembered how he had given Leroy Jordan's sweatbands to Big Willis and how proud Big Willis was of him.

Trey watched the screen as he and Big Willis walked off the field. Big Willis turned around and waved goodbye directly into the camera.

Trey cried.

The Heights

The street baseball game ended. Radio and Fat's team won again. This time the score was 13-5 when Fat ended the game. With a mighty swing of his meaty arms, Fat busted the well-worn rubber ball with the mop handle that substituted for a baseball bat. The ball split into two pieces, one piece flying off to the right toward Don Charles' yard and the other flying off to the left toward Onion Head's yard, leaving the fielders of Don Charles' team confused as to which piece of shattered rubber to chase.

Fat, a hulking thirteen-year-old, rumbled down the middle of the street touching the water main base in front of his Uncle Ervin's house, and then hustled back to the other water main that served as home plate. He laughed the whole way. Radio and his teammates laughed as well.

"Game over," Radio announced. "We got to get another ball."

Rosalind Heights in the 1960s was a kid-friendly neighborhood built for black families outside the city limits of Birmingham. There were no parks and no ball fields. The children played in the street, and parents drove their cars carefully so as not to harm any of them. For most of the children, it was a fun place to grow up.

The boys and girls of 86th Street moved like a swarm of bees to the four squares drawn in chalk on the blacktopped street in front of Radio's house. Radio dispatched his younger sister to get the bigger Foursquare ball, and a game broke out.

Radio and Fat again teamed up. The teams rarely changed. Radio and Fat were inseparable as a team.

Radio's sister, Tracey, a year younger than Radio, could play on his team if she promised not to play like a girl. Radio was all about winning. To play on Radio's team, you had one goal and that was to win.

Foursquare was a game the girls could play with the boys. Four squares were drawn onto the blacktopped street with a crayon rock. Crayon rocks, plentiful in Rosalind Heights, made perfect chalk lines—just like real chalk—on the street. One person occupied a square. The person who advanced to the server's square served the ball. The ball could only bounce once in a respective square before you had to move it along to someone else.

Moving it along for a seasoned Foursquare player could mean a slam shot, a two-handed slam, a twist shot, or a spin shot that was almost impossible to hit because it spun back to the person who hit it and away from the person in the square.

Don Charles, Goose, Onion Head, Truck, and Cynthia formed the other team. At fourteen, Don Charles was the oldest and the biggest of the group. He liked having his own team and was envious of Radio, which led to fights between him and Fat. Fat, who didn't have a good home life, considered Radio's family his own.

The other players, boys and girls, were ages ten through twelve, including JuneBug, Fat's stepbrother.

JuneBug was the opposite of his stepbrother. Fat was big, burly, and rough. JuneBug was the one player no one wanted on his or her team. JuneBug might one day be a rocket scientist, but at ten years old and left-handed, he couldn't play spit.

In choosing teams for baseball, the all-important hands-over-the-bat player draft, with the last hand hanging on to the bat's top, was critical. Whoever won the first choice was also assured they would not have the last choice. If Radio won the first choice, it was always Fat. The last choice was always JuneBug.

In football, JuneBug's assignment never changed. In the huddle, after all the assignments had been given out, it was, "Go down to Mrs. Bessie's mailbox and hook and I'll fake it to you." JuneBug would ask the quarterback, "What do you want me to do?" "You hike," was always the curt response.

JuneBug had an edge though. He owned most of the sporting equipment the kids played with. His dad bought all the gloves, bats, and balls for the neighborhood. The kids couldn't play without JuneBug.

It was Radio's mom who introduced the kids to the game of Foursquare because it was a game both girls and boys could play together. She had played it as a child, and the kids loved when she played, all except Radio. He didn't like playing with his mom. "It's not fair," he told her. "Who wants to play with their mom?"

"Hey, everybody!" screamed Michael Cooper, who lived down the street in the Addams Family house. The Cooper's house was filthy and dirty, with at least ten cats and dogs walking in and out at all times, leading to the nickname, Addams Family house, after the television show.

"Somebody's moving in on the back road, and they got kids," Cooper exclaimed.

Screech! The game came to an abrupt halt. This had to be investigated. Radio, in full gait, raced through Don Charles' yard, the short cut to 85th Street. The others followed in full flight looking like a cross-country team.

"Who is it?" Son, Don Charles' younger brother, wanted to know.

"How do you think I know, dummy?" Don Charles scolded him.

Son shrugged. "Okay. You don't have to call me a dummy."

"But you are," again scolded his older brother.

They ran until they came to the new house.

Someone was moving in all right. A big raggedy truck with wooden side rails and tires that were half flat, sat in front of the new house. The raggedy truck contained beds, a refrigerator, a washer, and sofas. A second truck, a pickup, was overloaded with clothes, books, bicycles, and whatnot.

They were moving into the latest house to be constructed on 85th Street. It was brown with three bedrooms upstairs and a full basement, with enough room for a family car, another bedroom, and plenty of storage space.

All the houses on 85th Street were new. Eighty-fifth was the continuation of the build out of the neighborhood, and even though it came before 86th in numerical order, it was considered the back road because 86th had been there longer.

From the bicycles and other toys in the pickup, it was obvious the new people had children. They had lots of children. Standing around, or helping with the move-in, were eight youngsters. There was an older teenage girl, and to Radio's delight, there were five boys—two of them close to Radio's age.

Radio's group stood around but stayed out of the way of the men moving boxes and furniture into the house. They knew to stay out of grown folks' affairs. Radio ventured in to talk to the new kids. The new mother, eager to get the children out of her hair, told them they could go and meet the neighborhood youth. All the kids started jumping up and down, excited. It was on!

Radio introduced everyone all around and gave the new Miller kids the lay of the land. The boy Radio's age was named Cool. No one said why. But Cool was okay by everyone in Radio's group. The next oldest boy was called Them. Again, no one asked, and there was no explanation. Cool and Them were twelve and ten, the right age as far as Radio was concerned.

Radio, earning his nickname, talked up a blue streak right there in the middle of 85th Street. He told the newcomers about 86th Street and his hill as he called the hill, where they all lived.

The Millers revealed that they had moved from across town and had gone to a school with a band, track team, and music lessons. No one in the Heights had been that exposed. The county school they all attended was a throwback to yesteryear. There was no band, no sports teams, nothing. The books handed out annually had been previously used by children in white city schools. During segregation, books for black students came ragged, used, and with the names of the former owners in them. Radio remembered one name, the one in his history book. It was Willis Williams III, "Trey." Radio wondered, *Who was Trey? Where did he live?* Radio often wondered about life outside of Rosalind Heights.

Radio explained to the Millers about Mr. McCloud, who was the meanest man in the neighborhood. If, during the street football game, the ball rolled into Mr. McCloud's yard and nestled on his pretty green lawn, the game was over until Mr. McCloud decided to give the ball back. The ball would sit on his luscious lawn, and no one would dare go to get it.

Radio told the new kids how Mr. McCloud was the eyes and ears of the neighborhood. Mr. McCloud, a wiry man, was retired from the railroad because of a disabling eye injury. He had one good eye and within the other eye socket sat something that looked like a big brown marble. The marble never moved.

"One time . . ." Radio began, and he told of the time when four drunk white boys had come screaming up the hill in a two-toned Mercury and hollered out the window at Radio and the others screaming, "Niggers! Niggers!"

It was strange to see white boys in the Heights. They had to have been lost. Those white boys did not have any idea Mr. McCloud lived on that hill. Nor did they know that 85th Street ran into a dead end.

Radio and company got the last laugh. Mr. McCloud, in his yard as always, took the insults to heart and sprang into action. He pulled his long, black, funeral-looking Coupe de Ville Cadillac across the road blocking the white boys' exit. The boys, terrified, had nowhere to go. The only alternative was to turn around and face Mr. McCloud and his long, ancient, double-barreled shotgun.

The Miller kids' eyes got big.

"Did he kill them?" one of the younger girls wanted to know.

"No," Radio relayed. "Mr. McCloud is mean, but he won't hurt anybody. He stared those boys down with his good eye. Then, he popped out his false eye and held it up as though it was looking at the boys too. They were scared out of their minds. He told those boys, 'I don't bother anybody, and I don't want anybody bothering the children on this hill or me. Do you understand?' The shotgun looked almost as tall as he was. They understood."

"Mr. McCloud popped his eye back in, turned to us, and winked with his good eye. The marble eye, back in place, did not move. He finally agreed to let those boys ride off down the hill."

"And you better not speed," he warned them. "You might hit one of these children."

"They never came back," Radio finished.

"Who's the fastest?" Them impatiently interrupted. "Cool ran track at our old school."

Tracey, Radio's sister jumped in. "Radio is the fastest boy in the Heights."

Them countered, "Cool was the fastest at our whole school."

"He ain't faster than Radio," Fat chimed in.

"Cool is the fastest," one of Cool's younger sisters bragged.

"Radio is the fastest in the world," Tracey bragged on her brother.

Radio threw out the challenge. "Let's race," he said to Cool.

"Okay," Cool accepted without hesitation.

"From pole to pole," Fat announced.

The race would be from one telephone pole to the other, about forty yards. The boys lined up in the middle of the street. The others gathered on either side of the street, Radio's supporters on one side and Cool's on the other. Word spread like brushfire on the hill that Radio was racing the new fellow. Other kids gathered.

Cool got down in a track starter stance. No one in the Heights had ever seen a live track stance. Sure, they'd seen them on television in the Olympics, but never live. Radio got down in a crude street stance.

Fat counted it off. "Ready. Set. Go!"

The boys took off like colts out of a starting gate. Radio jumped ahead to the delight of his crowd. They screamed and shouted. "Yay! Yay! Yay!"

Cool, his oversized thighs churning, raced just behind Radio and then leaned ahead. Radio alarmed, shifted into another gear. No one had ever come close to beating Radio.

Radio willed himself back alongside Cool.

The two boys, arms and legs moving like pistons, fought neck and neck. In the last five yards of the race, Cool pulled ahead and won!

"Yay! Yay! Yay!" came the cries from Cool's side of the street. "Yay! Yay! Yay!"

Radio's side of the street was quiet, stunned. No one had ever beaten Radio. Fat ran to Radio, so did the others.

Radio's entourage looked to him for answers.

"What happened?" Fat wanted to know.

Radio rubbed his legs, dumbfounded. He'd never been beaten. Obviously something had to be wrong somewhere. Radio checked his shoes.

"Let's race again," Radio challenged.

"Yeah!" Radio's supporters yelled.

"We dare you," Tracey scoffed in support of her brother.

"Double-dog dare you," Fat chimed in.

This time Radio took off his shoes. This time he meant business.

No one could come close to Radio when he ran barefoot. "Let's go farther," Radio announced.

"Yeah," Fat agreed. "From this pole to the far pole." The distance would double to about eighty yards. Everyone agreed.

Fat counted them off again. "Ready. Set. Go!"

Radio shot out of his crude stance but was already behind as Cool had gotten out smoothly and was sailing along.

Radio dug down. He caught Cool and looked at him as he passed him. Radio's crowd went crazy. "Yay! Yay! Yay!"

Cool lowered his head, strained his muscles, and accelerated past Radio.

Radio fought back. He grunted and dropped his shoulders, gaining speed. His flat feet flapped against the pavement.

Radio moved ahead. Then Cool. Radio. Cool. Radio.

Then…

Cool nipped Radio at the pole.

Radio's side of the street fell silent. Cool's side erupted, the Miller kids rubbing it in. "Yay! Yay! Yay!" They were now officially a part of the up the hill crowd.

Radio looked sheepish but quickly regained control.

"Okay let's play football," Radio announced.

Everyone converged onto the middle of the street, JuneBug first. As usual, Fat fell in beside Radio and their customary teammates.

"Okay," Radio declared to Cool, "You're with me and Fat."

Cold, Hard Grits

"Tommy! Tommy?! Is that boy still asleep? I swear!" Already into her early Saturday morning to-do-list of cooking, cleaning, and fussing over her family, she tried one more time. "Tommy!" she shouted.

Not a peep.

The delicious smell of frying bacon filled the air. Annoyed, Mom walked swiftly toward the bunk beds, located in the back room of the house. "Tommy?" She shook him. "Will you get up? Breakfast is on the table, and everyone is waiting on you."

He didn't move a muscle. Twelve and growing like a newly fertilized weed, his size eight feet hung over the edge of the bunk.

"Your breakfast is on the table." Next came Mom's direst warning. "If your grits get cold, you'll still have to eat them."

She rushed from the room, a grin slicing across her face.

As soon as his mom cleared the doorway, Tommy sprang from the bed, bounded across the guardrail, and landed. Feet planted nimbly on the floor, he wiped ten hours of sleep from his eyes. Tommy shut his door, jumped out of his pajama bottoms, pulled the top over his head, and slipped into blue jeans and a T-shirt. Barefoot, he rushed into the bathroom to brush his teeth. He splashed water on his face. Tommy checked himself in the mirror. He was ready!

"If your grits get cold..." Mom's words hung like a cloud over his head, "...you'll still have to eat them."

He hurried into the dining room.

"Morning, everybody," he said. His dad and two sisters were hungrily devouring the hot and tasty Saturday morning breakfast. Bacon, ham, grits, eggs, toast, and pancakes; the trusty jar of Alaga syrup stood nearby, its contents available to sweeten up the morning. Dad, coffee cup in hand, had his face buried deep into the morning newspaper. His thick-knotted fingers reached for the last piece of bacon from a nearly empty plate.

Older sister Tracey smiled at her younger brother. Baby sister, Myko, greeted him happily, "Good morning, Jr.!"

Mom pointed to Tommy's full plate. "Let it get cold, and you're still going to have to eat it all. And next time wash your face and put some shoes on."

Silence. The Saturday morning ritual had begun.

Tommy eyed the grits, ham, eggs, and pancakes on his plate. He cut into the ham, reached for the bacon, and shoved some pancake into his mouth.

Mom and Dad made weekend breakfasts a priority, the only day the family ate breakfast together. After a busy week of work and school, it was good family time. Time to catch up on events from the past week and anything new that might be coming.

"My school is going to the zoo next week," Myko declared.

"That's good, baby," Dad spoke, chewing the rest of his bacon.

"Make sure you ride the train," Tracey instructed. "You better get going on those grits," she chided her younger brother.

Tommy gave his sister the "I'll get you later look." Tracey smirked.

Tommy blew through ham, bacon, eggs, and pancakes. His stomach grew to cantaloupe size. He looked around for more.

"There is no more," Mom declared. "Eat the grits."

The ominous grits lay there, thickening into a cold, hard clump. *Ugh!*

Tommy hated grits. Hated them! They just did not suit his taste buds. He had eaten them when he was younger. Hot grits with melted butter weren't bad. But, because he didn't like them, Tommy always let them sit until they were no longer hot, until they got cold and turned into hard clumps of goo. The thought made him frown. When he turned ten, he swore off them. *No more.* He refused to eat them anymore. "No," he would silently say to himself. But Mom, the Supreme Being in the household, always overruled him. It was a tug-of-war that Tommy always lost. If needed, Mom would bring out the big guns—Dad, who would give Tommy "The Look." The Look would end the grits war for that Saturday.

Time slowed. Mom waited. Tommy tapped his fork on his plate.

Mom ignored him. It was his move.

He ate a piece of fruit.

Mom didn't break her stony countenance. Tommy raised his fork and pushed the grits from one end of his plate to the other. Now hard, they moved in one congealed clump.

"Go on," his mom urged.

With his mom watching, Tommy loaded a large clump of grits and guided them into his mouth. They were cold and hard. Bad taste alarms shot off all through his body. His face wrinkled up like a Sherpa. His eyes watered. He wanted to spit the grits out but knew better. He looked around the table for sympathy. With a mouth full of grits he begged, "Aw, Ma."

Mom sat stone-faced. Tommy washed the grits down with a large glass of water. "Ma," he pleaded again.

"I'm done," she announced. She left the room. The job of enforcer had now been turned over to Dad.

Dad's head and eyes never left the newspaper.

"Eat the grits. They're good for you." Dad's clipped tone spoke volumes.

Tommy tried an opening. "I know they're good for me, so I'll eat them next time, when they are hot. Okay, Dad? I've eaten everything else."

Dad explained. "You want to be a football player, you have to eat grits. They're good for you. Make you strong."

"But Dad," Tommy tried.

Dad's tone ended the discussion. "Eat the grits!"

Tommy, earning his nickname—Radio—kept up the chatter. "Daddy, so what was work like this week?"

His dad didn't answer.

Tommy continued. "You know, we got a big game today, Uphill against Downhill. I'm ready."

No response from his dad.

"I got all the plays written out. Gonna kill 'em."

Dad raised his head from the newspaper, giving Tommy The Look. The time for talk was over.

Tommy pouted, sulked, and continued pushing around the clump of grits. He loaded a spoonful, and for his dad's satisfaction, dramatically dropped the clump into his mouth. The round lump of grits slid down his throat past his Adam's apple, landing in his stomach. Tommy's face registered the foulness of their taste. He wanted to throw up. He looked to his dad.

Dad got back to his newspaper and the sports section. Tracey and Myko cleaned the table. Mom did the dishes. Tommy tried another tact. "Dad, who won the Dodgers game?" Tommy asked. Dad was a Dodgers fan. He relished telling how the Dodgers had won the game, or what they'd done to blow it.

"The Dodgers won," Dad answered.

Tommy rested his fork. "That's great," Tommy chimed in.

Dad held up his hand, cutting Tommy off. "Last time," he reminded. "I've got work to do. Eat. The. Grits." Dad took his watch off and set it on the table. Time ticked away as Tommy's grits got harder.

Tommy understood the symbolism of the watch. He now had five minutes to finish the clump of grits or... face the wrath of his parents' punishment. Tommy's parents never hit him. They believed in punishment. They would take away something he valued. They would refuse to let him go out and play today. That meant no game today! That meant Tommy's team would lose without him. Oh No! Punishment would not do. Tommy would rather have been beaten. Whippings were over quickly. They never hurt much. Tommy knew his parents would never hurt him. With a whipping, he could cry a few crocodile tears and be out on the street playing in the next ten minutes. But Tommy's parents didn't play it that way.

Tommy would miss the weekend football showdown, the Uphill vs. Downhill game of the week.

His options didn't look good. It was either eat the grits or be in the house, face pressed against the glass living room window pane, watching his guys get creamed, all because of those darn grits.

I hate grits, Tommy thought.

Taking one for the team, he closed his eyes and dumped a spoonful of the cold mush into his mouth. He swallowed the clump whole. Water flowed from his eyes.

"No pity in the naked city," his dad said.

"Tom?" Mom called her husband from the washroom down the hall, "Will you help me in here?"

Dad grumbled, giving Tommy one last look that warned, "When I get back the grits had better be gone." He stood over Tommy making sure he was understood. Tommy understood. Dad left. Tommy set about disposing of the grits.

When Dad returned Tommy was forcing down the last mouthful. He'd beaten the watch. He'd be playing in the game today. Tommy carried his plate into the kitchen.

Dad patted his son on his head, "Don't forget to feed the dog."

In the kitchen, Mom inspected Tommy's plate. "I knew you wanted to play today," she said.

Tommy, defeated, walked out the kitchen door with the plate of leftover table scraps. *If he wouldn't wait until the grits got cold,* his mom thought, feeling sorry that they had been hard on their son.

Tommy called the dog, "Tippy! Tippy!"

Tippy broke from his doghouse, bounding toward his morning breakfast. He bounced up on his hind legs, mouth open, sniffing and smelling the leftovers Tommy carried. "Wait now," Tommy urged.

Tippy wouldn't back off. His Saturday morning meal was late. Tommy poured the scraps into the dog's bowl and stepped back, as Tippy furiously gobbled them, inhaling them. In seconds, Tippy was licking his plate and panting. He expected more.

No one was looking. Tommy bent down and emptied his pockets. The clumps of grits fell into the dog's pan. Tommy scraped the grit crumbs from his pocket.

In seconds, Tippy devoured the cold, hard grits.

Everybody's Crazy

The moon slowly shifted its full face to the left of my position. I crept out of its bright light and further into the black of night. Darkness brought cover, and as always, her warning. All hell could break loose at any minute. Mortars, gunfire, grenades, and IEDs could light up the night like the Fourth of July.

I tingled inside with excitement.

The streets were clear with the exception of the two boys playing across the street. I slid further into the clump of trees in Mr. Burke's yard. Better cover for me. The boys couldn't see me. I would be here until dawn.

I had guard duty.

I took my position. I was ready. The quiet evening was peaceful and uneventful so far. *Don't relax*, I reminded myself.

Screeching tires jerked my attention. I jerked my weapon up, aimed, ready to fire.

Young Hardy, the best shade tree mechanic in the Heights, turned his two-toned, '57 Chevy onto 86th Street, driving like a madman. I had him in my sights. One squeeze of the trigger, a shot to the head is all I would need. *Crazy fool*, I thought. *Could get somebody killed.*

Leaves crackled to my left. I shifted, weapon at the ready. It was Ole Blue, one of Mr. Burke's sorry ass hunting dogs. Blue had never hunted anything but food scraps. He wouldn't chase a cat. Wouldn't run if you threw a rock at him. He'd just lazily sidestep it. But Mr. Burke loved that dog. Blue was his buddy.

For some reason, tension sizzled in my body. I was intense. If I was still over there, I'd shoot Blue's ass. The thought of killing Ole Blue made me smile. I stroked my weapon. I checked the gun's magazine. I was locked and loaded.

I took a long pull on the joint of weed I'd gotten earlier.

I'd never smoked weed until I got over there. Weed numbed the pain. Weed helped eighteen to twenty-two year olds deal with death. Weed helped with the guilt of killing. Weed, bonded black and white boys who'd never had to bond before. I took another long pull, held the smoke in my lungs, and took off for the night sky.

"Ah! That hurts!" The voices carried in the night air. They came from across the street. The two boys wrestled in a freshly raked pile of leaves. The bigger boy rode astride the smaller one, pulling at his curly hair. The little guy, like a cartoon hero, slipped underneath the bigger guy and mounted him. They rolled laughing and playing in the mountain of leaves. I thought, *Their parents must be crazy, letting them out after dark.*

The moon was now directly overhead. The man in the moon looked down on me but he wasn't smiling. He hadn't smiled in a while. What was there to smile about?

They spied me. *Shit.* The boys were laughing at me. They always laughed at me. They were pointing at me and laughing — loud. Everyone in the neighborhood laughed at me. They all said I was crazy.

I pretended I didn't see them.

I had been the nerd, special class. "The short bus," they joked. My brother had always called me a dummy. I never had a girlfriend. Angie Brown laughed at me when I fell down the steps during the school assembly. That's why I volunteered — to show them, to let them all know I was not stupid. I was not the old Son. Son, the dummy, the one everybody laughed at.

The day after I graduated from high school, I signed up. Three months later, having never been further than the 150 miles to basic training in Columbus, Georgia, having never flown on a plane before, having never had a white man as a friend, I landed in a country I'd never known existed except for the evening news.

Sarge told us we were there to fight for their freedom. I believed him.

The boys rose up and pointed at me. They disappeared, running and giggling behind the Beecher's home.

Were they armed?

Children could be armed over there! Children could be walking, ticking bombs. That's why we couldn't defeat them. No one in this country is going to blow him or herself up because they believe in something.

Over there, you had to guess. Friend or foe? It was crazy. Your life depended on it. They hid. They dug tunnels underground. They lived among us. It was complicated. Many had come to the states after the war. The last thing I was told in my debriefing was that the people here in the states are confused as to whom the enemy was.

Walking through the airport, on the way home, I was the enemy. They spit on me. Called me a baby killer. I didn't react. They didn't know any better. They believed Jane Fonda. They were helping the enemy. They say they want peace. Don't they know you have to kill for peace?

"They won't understand," were the last words of the captain. "Try not to upset them. They're all living high on the life you have created for them."

After two tours during my three-year stretch, it was obvious things were different when I returned. Sgt. Drake wanted me to reenlist. Sarge had been my dad. I smile when I think of him. He called me one of the finest fighting machines he'd ever run across. That meant a lot coming from Sarge. I wasn't a dummy. I wasn't Son. I was Jimmy—a killing machine.

We were considered an elite group. We removed things. People, villages, politicians; whoever or whatever. If the odds were against a soldier having any reasonable chance of getting back safely, Sarge would choose me, and I'd gladly accept.

I tried to reenlist, but they wanted me out. The counselors and doctors wanted me out. The Army wanted me out. They determined I was more dangerous in than out.

They tried to prep me in the hospitals. Get me ready for life back in the States. The doctors played crazy mind games with books and videos. I bonded with Frank from Massachusetts. Frank and I would hide the pills they gave us under our tongues and later flush them down the toilets. We gave the doctors the answers they wanted to hear. All the time we kept petitioning to go back. We had to convince them of our sanity because only sane people were allowed to go to war.

The doctors sent me home.

My mind flashes to Terry. Always, I think of Terry.

Terry's screams are a part of my life, imbedded in me. They killed Terry in front of me, his chest blown open, and his blood squirting into my eyes. I held him, begged him not to die. Now, his screams keep me awake. But, I never shed a tear, not then, not now.

I started to smoke the weed.

Sarge treated me special, but he didn't approve of me smoking weed. He did come to understand it numbed me, fueled my courage, and made me sane in the middle of an insane world. I'd never seen it until I got there. I hadn't been without it since.

That's where I first got the idea of being buried in Glenwood Cemetery—from Sarge. Glenwood was the finest cemetery in Birmingham. It sat in the middle of a black neighborhood. I grew up not far from there. It was immaculate; the cream of Birmingham was buried there if you were white. Sarge told me to make out a will, just in case. I wrote that I wanted to be the first black person buried in Glenwood Cemetery. I also wanted a twenty-one-gun salute. That made me smile. Hell, if I was going to die for some people's freedom in another country, I was damn sure going to be buried where I wanted to be buried. Sarge said, "Okay."

"Jimmy?" It was my mama's voice. I crawled into position. Mama couldn't possibly understand.

There had been nights when I knew Mama was afraid of me, the screams in my sleep and night sweats. She wanted me out of the house. The lack of fear in me kept her up at night. I was not the same Son who had grown up slow and nervous. I was Jimmy, dammit! I had killed people. She always asked if I was taking my meds.

I'd lie and say yes. I hid my weapon from her.

Crawling through the clump of leaves close to Mr. Burke's house, I thought of the swamps and fields we crawled in over there. *Be careful.* There had been mines, snipers, and snakes. I settled in behind Mr. Burke's shrubbery. I was safe.

Mr. Burke understood me. He liked me, took time with me, and talked to me. He was like a dad. But not like the dad Sarge had been. Sarge made me a man.

"Son…? Son?" she was still calling. She was calling me that name. *I'm Jimmy!* I wanted to scream.

I hated having to bunk with my mom. War makes no sense!

I felt for my weapon. Seductively, I stroked it.

The sting of the sharp rock against my head brought stars. I was woozy for a moment. Warm drops of blood dripping into my eyes brought excitement. *The enemy is attacking!* They bolted from their cover! There were two of them, running toward the street, toward me. Laughing!

Gooks! Adrenaline raced inside me. My heart leaped. I heard Terry's screams, felt his blood! *Shit!*

I opened up on them.

They fell.

In the streetlight glow, their bodies were ripped and torn.

I advanced my position carefully, while reloading. They could be booby-trapped.

They looked a lot like the little Harris kids down the block. Yes they did! Damn, this was confusing! Looking up, I saw Mr. Burke and Mrs. Beulah running toward me.

Mrs. Harris was running and screaming.

Mama ran toward me. Her look filled with fear and hysteria. She was calling out, "Jimmy?! Jimmy?!"

This was embarrassing! Why was Mama here?

They were all crying.

This is war. Don't they know that?

What the hell was wrong?

Everybody's crazy, I thought.

Just Like Television

"I'll go first," Buck instructed. "Then Chris, come in. Tyrone, you hang around outside near the door. Don't cause no suspicion now. Got it?" Buck, from the drivers' seat, stared at Tyrone in the rear view mirror.

Chris, from the passenger seat, waited for Tyrone's answer.

Tyrone nodded but without conviction.

Quiet and darkness set in inside the car as Buck settled the Blue Camaro onto the exit ramp of the freeway. They began their descent into the city.

Tyrone's full stomach felt queasy. Buck had insisted they eat on the way to the job. He stopped at Church's Chicken® on Martin Luther King Boulevard, got a family box of greasy chicken, dinner rolls, corn on the cob, and ate it in the parking lot of the fast food restaurant. Tyrone ate a wing and couldn't eat anymore. He had no appetite.

Buck devoured the drumsticks, breasts, two ears of corn, two dinner rolls, sucked down a 24 oz. strawberry soda, and belched a sinful, nasty, loud, vulgar belch then said, "Let's do this."

They rolled toward the western side of town.

Anticipation gripped Tyrone in the darkness of the back seat. His chest was tight, his throat dry. His 6'1" frame hardly fit into the tight back seat of the sports car. He slumped and bent his head forward to find some comfort for his long legs.

Tyrone's long legs had carried him to the 400-meter state finals in high school. "Little Horse," they called him. He finished second, but no scholarship offers came his way. He had no money for further education.

I've been to this store many times before. The thought drifted across Tyrone's brain. The car hit a bump in the worn road. The coldness of the blue steel in Tyrone's pants touched his skin. This ride to the store was different. He knew it. He removed the gun from inside his pants and placed it on the seat, pointing it away from himself and toward Buck

Tyrone had tried to get his old high school buddy Goose to come along. He'd begged Goose, but Goose begged off. "Ain't going to jail, Jack," Goose responded.

Approaching the destination, Tyrone could see the blinking lights of the 7-11®. The city streets were naked, with the exception of an old, fat bag lady wobbling her way home from the bus stop and a day of scrubbing, cleaning, and caring for someone else's home and children. She walked as though her feet hurt, and her next step would be her last. A step, a wobble; she would shift her weight then take another step, another wobble. Tyrone thought, *Everyone has to make a living.*

Buck had instructed that they all wear black windbreakers and a black cap just like he'd seen the bad guys do on *CSI-NY*, his favorite show. "Zip up," Buck commanded.

Sweat beads gathered on Tyrone's forehead. Even though it was a warm night, cold chills crept into his bones. Was this the dumbest thing he'd ever done? How could he get out of it? Was he scared of Buck? He was damn sure afraid of Chris. What about his family?

He'd married Pam two weeks ago. It felt good to marry the mama of his two-year-old son. He promised to get a job and help her with the bills. A good woman, Pam worked as a nurse. She was smart with money. She and Tyrone had dated since high school. She had gotten pregnant their senior year.

He thought of his son. Little Man, they called him. Tyrone had been so proud the day he was born. He'd held him so close, those first few days. He'd vowed to do right by his son. He tried. He drove cabs. He did day labor. He'd landed a career opportunity loading trucks with UPS®. Thirty days later, they fired Tyrone for a positive marijuana test. He hadn't worked in a year. Desperate, he tried to make nice with his father long enough to get his rent covered. Daddy said, "No way. When I tried to help you, you didn't want it." His father had arranged a job for Tyrone in the steel plant where he'd worked for forty years, but Tyrone turned it down. "I ain't working in no plant," he emphatically told his father the last time they had talked.

Buck's gruff voice interrupted Tyrone's thoughts. "Get ready." Buck, at nineteen, was a convicted felon and a violent veteran criminal. He slowed to make the right turn into the parking lot but then suddenly accelerated and passed his mark. No one said anything. Tyrone breathed a little easier. Both Tyrone and Chris had faith in Buck. Tyrone thought, *Buck's the man. He knows what he's doing.*

Buck circled the block, making sure there were no cops around. He came back and made his turn. The lot was vacant. The store was empty of customers. Chris reached over and killed the radio.

Buck pulled the Camaro next to the rectangular building with flashing neon lights. Only the old man was inside, just as Buck had figured and Tyrone had said. Tyrone hit the illuminating dial on the watch Pam had given him, 10:49. Buck turned, checked his piece of big, cold blue steel, and demanded, "Everybody be cool. It'll be over in three minutes. Don't be a fool."

Buck opened the door, slid from under the wheel, and made his way around the car. He shoved the gun into the back of his pants just like criminals did on television. Chris followed. He shoved his gun down into the back of his pants, just like Buck. Tyrone lingered for a few precious seconds. He'd begun to sweat and beads of water trickled down his forehead, into his eyes. He thought about running. Just running. Maybe, running track again. When he was running track, it had been the happiest time of his life.

"Damn," he murmured.

The night air was thick, the heat a forewarning of trouble. Water beaded up on Tyrone's forehead and ran from under his arms. Like Buck and Chris, Tyrone tucked the gun into the back of his pants.

He started for the door about the time he figured Buck and Chris were inside. Tyrone was the lookout. He was afraid, afraid to go through with it and afraid to leave.

Tyrone could see the old man, Mr. Perkins. He knew Mr. Perkins through his grandfather, who also worked at this store. Tyrone had casually mentioned that his grandfather, his father's father, worked at a 7-11®, and Buck had taken it from there. Tyrone had protested, but Buck reasoned it was all the way across town and their heads would be covered. No one would get hurt. He swore it would be a piece of cake. Tyrone stood his ground and insisted the job be done when his grandfather was not working.

Tyrone peeked inside the store. He did not want Mr. Perkins to see him.

Mr. Perkins had retired from his job in the factory. His wife had died five years before. He worked in the 7-11® to make a few bucks and get out of the house. Tyrone's grandfather had recommended him to the owner, who hired him. Mr. Perkins stood slightly slumped and his hair grew in gray patches throughout his head. His customers loved him and his pleasant disposition. He, in turn, enjoyed his interaction with his customers.

Looking through the glass, Tyrone lost his focus. Mr. Perkins reminded him of his grandfather. He pictured his grandfather standing behind the counter with Buck and Chris in the store. What would he do?

Tyrone snapped out of it, made it to his position. Buck, Chris, and Mr. Perkins were the only ones in the store. Things were moving smoothly. No problems.

Mr. Perkins did not see him.

Suddenly, without warning, the old man's eyes came alive, registering danger. He'd spotted the piece in the waistband of Chris's pants as Chris bent over pretending to look for some Oreo cookies. In a split second, Mr. Perkins, a kind, lovable older man, went under the counter for his piece, a Charter Arms Undercover .38 special.

Instantly, Buck, a veteran crook and felon with no dreams and no future at nineteen years old, went for his automatic, shouting, "He got a gun." Chris, having spent a few years in juvenile detention and having enthusiastically watched too many *Criminal Minds* episodes, dove spread eagle, behind the row of cookies.

Tyrone, paralyzed, watched it all unfold. He could not flee, nor could he help.

The old man fired the .38 special twice in Buck's direction. *Bam! Bam!*

Buck, kneeling, gun pointed sideways like he'd seen in the new rap video, fired multiple rounds. *Pop! Pop! Pop! Pop! Pop! Pop!*

It was surreal to Tyrone. It looked like television. The images were so vivid! The old man shooting, Buck behind the potato chip counter, and Chris lying prone on the floor, firing like a marksman. Tyrone thought about his own gun. The thought made him sick. This wasn't television. It was for real. His nervous stomach threw up the Church's Chicken® wing.

In the next instant, fate slammed the door on all four lives.

Buck rose, his gun sideways, and fired multiple times. The bullets caught Mr. Perkins full in the chest like target practice. Tyrone saw blood gush and squirt through the gray flannel work shirt. It wasn't like television at all. It wasn't surreal. It was real, bloody, and scary as hell. Bullets tore away at Mr. Perkins' flesh. Little pieces of his body flew in different directions. Mr. Perkins screamed out with the pain, became limp, and fell against the cash register, violently bumping his head. He hit the floor, lifeless.

It was time to go.

Tyrone's legs started moving. He pulled his gun, threw it toward the dumpster in the parking lot, and broke for the freeway. His stride was long and casual, but his heart and mind were frantic. He replayed the picture in his mind—Mr. Perkins' flesh being ripped open by the penetrating bullets. He tried blocking it but the pictures kept coming.

Sweat poured in currents from his body.

Tyrone ran. Running felt good. Running restored order to his world. He could control running. He started to relax. Running, he was able to think.

He didn't know if Mr. Perkins was dead or not. Yes he did. He knew Mr. Perkins was dead. *Damn!* He didn't look back for Buck and Chris. He never had to see them again, and it would be okay. He would never do this again. This had been stupid. He thought of Pam and Little Man. He was running to them. *I'm on my way honey. Hey, Little Man, Daddy is on his way home.* His thoughts raced along with him. *Maybe I'll call Daddy and get the job in the plant*, he thought. *Oh God, I hope so.*

Somehow, he ran up the entrance ramp to the freeway. Cars whizzed by. The thought of thumbing a ride entered his mind and exited just as fast. He continued running; his long strides now growing shorter; his breaths coming in fevered pants. He was no longer in running shape.

He never looked back. He didn't stop running. He never again wanted to stop running, never again.

Sirens whistled in the distance, and he knew cops must be on the scene. Never losing stride, he hit the watch dial, 11:00 pm. It was time for his grandfather's shift to start. Was his grandfather there? Would he find out? Would his dad?

Tired, exhausted, and run out, he wanted to quit running. He couldn't go anymore. He wanted to stop. He wanted to be in the little one-bedroom apartment with Pam and Little Man. He wanted the three of them to cuddle up in the bed his father had given him. He wanted to be home. Gradually, he slowed. Cars zipped by. He didn't look backward or to the side. He only wanted to look straight ahead. He stopped running. He didn't see or hear the Camaro pull up behind him. He didn't hear the horn blow. When he heard his name called, it startled him. He turned.

Buck pulled the Camaro next to him, and commanded, "Get in."

College Boy

"Well--ll, go 'head driver." Stumpy sang in the singsong language of garbage men plying their trade for the City of Birmingham in the 1970s. "I got it," the words flowed forcefully from his mouth.

Sweat poured from his stocky body, soaking his clothes.

Stumpy, the color of rich dark chocolate, was short, stocky, and muscular. His stomach protruded from his rock-hard body. Left-handed, he wore well-worn work gloves, a short sleeved button-up brown shirt and weary dark pants over his open, untied work boots. His hair was worn tight around his head. Stumpy had absolutely perfect white teeth, which he never used to smile.

Stumpy looked like a bad man!

He broke into a short-legged bouncy gait, his work boots clumping along on the blacktopped street. Gracefully, he hopped aboard the right side of the back of the truck, grabbed onto the handrail, threw his head back, and sang, "Drive the truck, Fred."

The raggedy, dented, and scratched green City of Birmingham garbage truck gagged, choked, shook, and rattled; leaked garbage juice from its hopper; farted a puff of choking, black smoke; and finally rolled forward.

Fred Love, the driver, checked the big rectangular mirror on the driver's side for any oncoming traffic. From my middle position on the back of the truck, I could see his white face and clear blue eyes in the mirror. Love guided the truck to the left side of the street, maneuvered around a parked car, and brought the truck to a crawl along the curb.

"Go 'head, man," Long Mouth Ricky scolded Love. "Drive the truck, Fred," he urged.

"Long Mouth Ricky" so named by Stumpy, commanded the left side of the truck. Ricky's yellowed teeth jutted from under his top lip in a poster child overbite. "Long Mouth, Duck Mouth, Mother Sucker," Stumpy would call him and throw his head back and laugh.

Ricky, slender, wiry, and more athletic than Stumpy, was also sixty pounds lighter. He didn't challenge Stumpy. Occasionally, he would playfully sneak up behind him, pop Stumpy with his open hand across the back of his head, and take off running like a sprinter, all the time laughing like a hyena. Stumpy would take a couple of steps in pursuit and decide there was no way he could catch Ricky. He would get him later, with a chokehold that could drop a bear.

Ricky, like a top athlete, leaped from the rolling truck, left leg extended horizontal to his body, and landed gymnast-like onto the ground. His momentum carried him to a full aluminum garbage can full of funky, foul, smelly garbage. Ricky pivoted, grabbed its handle, spun around, and swung the can high in the air, above his head, over, and into the truck hopper. "Yeah," he sang, his lips rising over his long teeth like Mr. Ed the talking horse. Beer cans, food wrappers, meat scraps, cereal, eggshells, tuna cans, and other garbage from the last three days slid from the can and into the truck's hopper. "Go 'head, driver." Ricky wiped the river of sweat from his forehead.

It was my first day as a garbage man and one I'd never forget.

The summer of 1968 had been Alabama tropical hot, but my summer job prospects had been Chicago cold. I had not been able to find a summer job and half of June was gone already. School and football practice would start in less than two months, and I needed money.

In previous summers, I'd worked selling ice cream from a truck, women's shoes downtown, and as a bus boy at Shoney's Big Boy® restaurant in Eastwood Mall. This summer I was coming up empty, but I was determined.

I'd leave home early morning Monday through Friday, armed with cutout classified ads for job openings. I'd even applied for a job as a controller, not knowing what it was but figuring I could control things. My parents were working class blue-collar blacks in Birmingham. Everyone they knew was in the same economic class. They did not have any contacts that could help.
I'd catch the bus downtown and spend the day looking for work.

"The city hires every Monday," Don Charles, my neighbor and friend, told me. Don Charles' name was Donald Charles Mayes. Everyone in the neighborhood called him Don Charles.

"Every Monday they hire garbage workers," Don Charles continued. "The guys get paid on Friday. Some of them get drunk all weekend and don't show up on Monday. They're automatically fired, and the superintendent hires new guys."

I'd never thought about working on a garbage truck.

The city's eastern sanitation office was a couple of miles from my house, walking distance.

"If you're hired on a garbage truck you only work four days a week. You're off on Wednesday."

Don Charles was a wealth of information.

"You start at 6:30 in the morning and you get off when you finish. If it's less than eight hours, you still get paid for eight."

The City was sounding better and better, especially when you're as broke as I was.

The past weekend, my buddies had caught the downtown bus without me. They'd gone shopping at the men's shops along Fourth Avenue in black downtown Birmingham. Blacks still were forbidden to travel much along the fine stores on Second and Third Avenues, so my friends had gone to the Carver, the downtown theatre for blacks, to see John Wayne as Colonel Mike Kirby in *The Green Berets*. It was the first film Wayne directed. Being broke, I'd had to miss The Duke kicking ass in Vietnam.

I also needed the money because I was going off to college in the fall, and any money I could make and save would be a big help to my parents, who were taking out loans to finance my education.

"You want to try it?" I asked.

"Okay," Don Charles answered.

Don Charles was a big guy, but he was not very assertive. The fact that we would go together boosted his courage. I was desperate.

I had passed the ugly green city building that housed dozens of ugly green city trucks and ugly green city equipment many times while riding home from the supermarket with my mom. I'd never imagined working there.

. . .

The scene that Monday morning was right out of a William Faulkner short story or maybe an old black and white photo from southern plantation slave days. There were about fifty black men in line, young men in their twenties and thirties without skills or education, and older men in their forties who needed to make the rent or buy the kid some shoes. Everyone was lined up outside alongside the building. Some were hung over. All seemed to have broken spirits with very little future to look forward to. Don Charles and I were the youngest. I hustled ahead of several other guys and ended up about ten bodies ahead of Don Charles.

We wondered what was next.

There was no application process. A lanky, pink colored, white man walked out of the office in a green city shirt and pants. He had the look of an alcoholic who had just had his last drink maybe an hour ago. His breath carried the smell of alcohol and mint. His green shirt read "Mr. Smith." He wore a little straw hat, with the front part of the hat turned down. His teeth were brown and he had the stub of a cheap cigar in his mouth. He was all business.

Like a plantation overseer, he ambled past the guys in front of me, eyeing them but not liking what he was seeing. Don Charles and I were two of the bigger guys in line. I was in excellent football condition at a hard one hundred and eighty pounds. I was trying out for the college football team in the fall and reasoned running behind a garbage truck could keep me in shape.

Mr. Smith stopped at me, looked me over and grabbed my shoulder, then squeezed my bicep. I expected him to check my teeth but he didn't. He grunted for me to step inside the office.

As I walked in, I saw him feel Don Charles up and down his upper torso and motion for him to come inside as well.

We were hired.

. . .

The truck rolled out of the City parking lot with Stumpy manning its right side, Ricky on the left side and me in the middle. Both sides had little perches for the end guys to stand on. They also had a handle. The slippery ledge across the back of the truck, bordering the hopper, was my standing place. There was no perch or handle.

The first bump in the road sent me flying into the air and hanging onto the back of the truck for dear life. Terrified, I desperately gripped the sharp back edge of the truck. The truck's metal dug deeply into my too-soft hands. Finally, I was able to get my feet back onto the ledge.

Stumpy cut his eyes to Ricky. They grinned.

When I left home that morning, I had no idea that I would be hired and start work the same morning. I was not prepared. I had on a nice shirt. I had no gloves, and instead of work boots, I wore basketball shoes. If I could make it through the day...

We rode through Eastern Birmingham on our way to the neighborhoods of Huffman and Center Point. Although these neighborhoods were less than five miles from my house, we never ventured there. To do so, we would have to cross the now invisible boundary of segregation, which was no longer illegal. Still, we knew these neighborhoods were for whites. Why cause trouble?

Love had the truck moving at a pretty good gait. Stumpy relaxed, holding onto the truck with one hand. He let the wind blow against his face, a regal presence on his green chariot.

Ricky pumped me for information. He found out I had gone to an integrated Catholic school and was going to a "white college." Since neither of them had been very far in school, Stumpy even quitting high school, I was nicknamed "College Boy."

Deep red creases dug into my hands from holding on so tightly to the truck. It hurt, but I didn't complain. I'd learned already that Stumpy did not tolerate complaining. "You should have known better than to show up at work with no gloves," he scolded me. I didn't.

The truck stopped for Love to run into a service station and take a pee. Stumpy walked to the front of the truck, opened the cab, and reached into his duffle bag on the truck's front seat. He pulled out an extra pair of worn work gloves and threw them to me. I caught them. "Thanks," I gratefully acknowledged.

Love walked out of the bathroom, zipping up his pants.

"Let's ride man,'" Stumpy commanded.

· · ·

Love wheeled the truck down a neighborhood street and slowed, bringing the vehicle to a crawl. Dozens of shiny and dulled aluminum cans were lined up and down the block, reflecting the early morning sun. They had been "set out" by Bear, another member of the team who was our "set out man." As the set out man, Bear drove ahead to the neighborhoods an hour and a half before we were scheduled to get there and went into the backyards of homes to get the full garbage cans and set them out on the curb. At 5:00 a.m., he sometimes fought startled and angry dogs, and on a couple of occasions, he tangled with startled and angry white men who were not familiar with the young brown skinned man coming into their backyard before day in the morning.

We would meet up with Bear at the end of our route.

"Hot Shot" was our "set back" man, meaning he set the cans back behind the house once they were emptied. Hotshot was easygoing, with brownish teeth and pink lips. He looked like a dark skinned Native-American with his round flat face. I recognized him instantly from the airport neighborhood close to where I lived. I remembered he had a large contingent of sisters and brothers. There were at least twelve of them. Stumpy kidded, asking him if he any brothers named "Raid."

I ran along behind the truck, being careful to watch for Stumpy and Ricky, wildly but skillfully swinging into the truck with a full can of garbage. With them it was a matter of pride not to spill any onto the ground. Most of the time they didn't. Spillage meant the truck had to stop and stopping would hurt our timing. If we hustled we could finish around 1:30 on Monday and Thursdays when we repeated the Monday route. On Tuesdays and Fridays we had a short route and could finish by 9:30 in the morning. Pushing it was also a way to beat the hottest part of the day.

"Two," Ricky grunted, as he ran to two cans on the left side of the truck. "Two" was my cue. It was time to go to work. I broke behind Ricky. Ricky stepped into the first can, pivoted, grabbed the can with his wiry body, swung it above his head, and spun. With a smooth shake of the can, held high over his head, the garbage flowed into the hopper within seconds.

I was not that smooth. I grabbed the can, and it did not move. It was full of watermelon, dead weight in a garbage can. Bees and flies feasted on the watermelon rinds. Love had to stop the truck. Stumpy gave me shit for that. The can was so heavy, I had to walk it with two hands to the back of the truck and hoist it into the hopper using my hands, arms, and legs and with the can balanced against my torso. Neither Stumpy nor Ricky would help me, but I knew Stumpy was watching me. I had to prove myself. The bees and flies swarmed all around my head. I got the trash into the truck's hopper.

We rolled on.

I watched and learned. Grabbing a can on the run required skill. You had to use the momentum of your body to hoist the can overhead, give it a good shake, hit it once against the hopper, and let the garbage fly. Then, you had to swing out of the truck hopper with the can and drop it off onto the sidewalk, never breaking stride while running to the next can. I wanted to get good at it like Stumpy and Ricky.

I liked the guys and I could tell they liked me, even though Stumpy played grumpy most of the time, enjoying calling me "College Boy" and Ricky, "Long Mouth."

"Welllll," Stumpy sang as we entered a new neighborhood.

White people lived in all the neighborhoods we worked. There was still no housing integration in Birmingham. We didn't have many incidents. We were garbage men, no threat to anybody. We were a necessity to the daily order of those people's lives.

The kids loved us. We passed a day care that was obviously familiar with Stumpy, Ricky, Love, and the green garbage truck. The kids ran to the fence waving and shouting, "Morning, Mr. Garbage Man. Hey, Mr. Garbage Man." Some of the kids ran along the fence trying to keep up with the truck. We waved back. We were big stuff to those kids.

I felt odd. I was riding on the back of a garbage truck, with guys I'd just met who I liked and white kids running to the fence to excitedly yell good morning to us. After the first couple of hours, I'd started to like being a garbage man but only for the summer.

"Got a jimmy." It was Ricky informing Love that he had a steel can one and one half times the size of a regular can and ten times as heavy. A "jimmy" took two guys to handle it. Love stopped the truck. Ricky and I grabbed the jimmy and crept it to the back of the truck. The jimmy was naturally heavy, and this one was also full of melon. We strained to get the can into the hopper.

Ricky hated jimmies. They slowed us down. But you couldn't hurt a jimmy like you could a regular aluminum can. If you slammed an aluminum can down hard or threw it back into the yard, it could bend and people would call up and complain. You couldn't dent a jimmy.

Ricky slammed the jimmy down, and we rolled on.

"Mucking time," Stumpy called out. "Stop the truck, man!" he shouted.

"It's time to muck."

Love looked into the long mirror on the right side of the truck. He wheeled the truck over to the curb. He put the truck into gear and applied the brake. The truck made a passing gas sound and stood steady. Love got out and came to muck.

Mucking happened when there was a large pile of trash with goods that were still usable. It was a chance to grab something to take home. The trash could include furniture, clothes, books, records, and any old discards. There would be very little garbage.

Love netted a couple of pairs of pants, Stumpy a clock, and Ricky a radio that worked. Stumpy found me a football. I accepted it. I wanted to fit in, but I couldn't bring myself to muck. I needed money for school and spending, but my parents took good care of our needs; mucking seemed beneath me at that time.

While out of the truck, Love chatted me up, getting to know me. He was interested in my high school. He congratulated me on going to college. He wanted to know my field of study. Love, like the others, had not gone to college. He had been drafted into the Army, and upon discharge, he landed the job driving a garbage truck for the city.

Love was the boss. We all knew in any labor situation involving a work crew, the white man was always the boss. But Love didn't hold himself above the guys working the truck. Love was cool. He laughed and joked with us. He allowed the guys to put their mucking bounty into the front of the truck. Love was one of the guys.

Mucking done, we rolled on.

We stopped at a little service station that fixed flats and gave tune-ups, and sat outside on used tires to have our lunch. Stumpy, Ricky, and Love had all brought their lunches. I had no lunch and no money. If only I had known. It was hot; I was dehydrated, hungry, and run down. At one time, I'd gotten light headed from running, perspiring, and no food or water. I fought to keep from passing out. But I would not complain. I would know better for tomorrow's run. I took a seat where I didn't have to watch them eat and avoided eye contact.

Stumpy was first. He shared a piece of fried chicken with me. Ricky bought me a soda. Love gave me a piece of cake. I thanked them, probably too much. They came over and sat next to me.

"You lucky you got on Love's truck," Ricky informed me. "Love a good man. He don't work you like a slave. Your buddy," he said referring to Don Charles, "got on Mueller's truck. Mueller is a slave driver. He gon' kill him if he can. All his guys end up quitting. Some don't make it one day. He drives that truck fast and won't take breaks. Needs a new crew every Monday." I felt bad for Don Charles and lucky that I was on Love's truck.

We were nearing the end of the day, and I was feeling pretty good. I was comfortable with the guys and Love. I was running, jumping, and playing (if you can call slinging garbage playing). I had not backed down from the challenge of not slowing the truck down.

Ricky was on the move. "Two." The word exploded from his mouth. Ricky broke for the two full cans on the left curb. I fell in behind him stride for stride. Synchronized garbage men, we grabbed the cans in tandem. Ricky swung first, bumping the tip of his can onto the hopper's edge, his garbage spilling from the can. He slid to his right out of my way as my garbage slid from the can I held high over my head.

"Well!" I hollered, taking Ricky's can in my free hand and setting the two cans back in front of 1952 Crestline Street, where we had found them.

"Well go 'head, driver," I sang. "Drive the truck, man." I was still a little self-conscious about the hollering and singing behind the truck, but I was getting there.

Around 12:30 we were done and heading for the dump.

. . .

The stench from the dump hit inside your nostrils like a funky tear gas. The smell slid down your throat and settled into your body, and you felt like you either needed the bathroom or were going to throw up. The awful, filthy taste stayed in your mouth, making this the worst part of the day. We bounced across two acres of garbage and filth until Love found a place to dump the day's garbage.

We stepped carefully from the back of the truck and into piles and piles of rank garbage. I drew the duty of walking through the slop in my basketball shoes and unlocking the levers on the truck that would allow the backside to rise into the air and the garbage to flow into the landfill. The truck unlocked, I waved Love on, "Go 'head, man," I said. Love pulled the truck forward and the garbage slid out of the truck and into the landfill. Love pulled the truck even further forward, freeing all of its garbage. The stench would stay with me through two baths and the rest of the day.

It was time to roll toward the garage.

We had been lucky. We'd only had to go to the dump once. On the day after the fourth of July there would be so much garbage we would go to the dump, out to pull more garbage, and back to the dump a second time.

With the truck empty of garbage, the only thing left was to get back to the lot and rinse the truck down. We rode back in silence, the wind whipping tears out of our eyes as we faced it.

I felt good, proud. I'd made it through the day as a garbage man.

Pulling garbage on the early morning drag had been a challenge to me. I'd used my athletic skills to last physically and my mental toughness to adapt, just like in football. I'd met the challenge.

Love and Stumpy agreed that Love would drop me off in East Lake on Eighty-Sixth Place, so I would not have to go all the way back to the lot. I could walk home from there.

It was an appropriate place. Eighty-Sixth Place was the dividing line between the white neighborhood of East Lake and the black neighborhood of Zion City. I could walk through Zion City to get home.

The truck slowed at Eighty-Sixth Place, my exit. Love did not slow enough, at least not enough for me to jump off. Stumpy and Ricky challenged me to jump from the moving truck. Love looked into the mirror, waiting. They all waited. It was all on me.

It was my last test of the day. To jump from the moving truck, land on my feet, and not topple head over heels.

"Too fast!" I told Stumpy and Ricky. "Tell him to slow down more." They laughed, Stumpy showing his rows of pretty white teeth and Ricky his extended yellow ones.

"College Boy says it's too fast," Stumpy hollered up to Love. Love laughed but slowed a little.

I jumped from the truck, hit the ground, and stumbled into a head first run. I regained my balance and broke into a comfortable gait, like I'd been jumping from garbage trucks all my life.

The guys, driving off into the distance, laughed and howled. They waved. I waved.

Excited, I yelled, "See you tomorrow!"

The First

"Last one!" screamed the beautiful bronze athlete, his skin glistening with sweat in the evening Birmingham sun.

He broke into a powerful and graceful jaunt, a restless stallion lurching from the starting gate. A gazelle of an athlete, gravel kicked backward from his fast-moving feet. In the backstretch of the oval 440-yard track, he dropped his buttocks and churning thighs into an even faster gear and sprinted home with a burst of speed and energy. At the imaginary finish line, he leaned forward like an Olympian.

"Good work," the old warhorse of a coach grunted.

The coach, whistle dangling across his chest and cap pulled down over his shaded eyes, limped alongside Danny. "You working hard. Expecting big things this year."

Danny, sweat pouring ripples over his lean muscled body, bent to stretch his oversized muscular thighs. "Yes, sir," he answered. He slid down into a split, stretched, and cooled down.

"Proud of you," the older man, who had seen it all, mumbled.

Their eyes met, one younger, one older, a generation apart. Coach Melvin Whitlark didn't give out compliments. The rare words of praise flew straight to Danny's heart. The understanding between the two went beyond coach and athlete. This was about the future.

Danny had been groomed for this. He'd dreamed of it. Others had dreamed of it for him. It wasn't just about football. It was his calling. Thousands of guys could play football. This was about change, moving society toward a new day, "a new South," they called it.

"The old way is gone," Whitlark would say. "The 1970s gonna be different."

Coach Whitlark knew all about the old South. He'd grown up in it. Survived it. Even thrived. He'd coached at the under-funded segregated schools in Birmingham all his life. He'd learned to do more with far less a long time ago. There was one other paid coach on his staff, the basketball coach. There were two volunteers from the neighborhood. One of the volunteers was "a little slow," as Coach Whitlark described his mental condition.

The equipment was second rate. The practice dummies were ripped open, with stuffing pouring out of them. There was little to no grass on the practice field. The boys had to buy their own shoes and were given used second-rate helmets and shoulder pads, discards from the white Birmingham city schools.

Whitlark did not yield. He demanded mental and physical toughness. "How bad do you want to play?" he would ask before the start of every fall camp. Those who couldn't handle Coach's physicality and his demands would quit. Their answer being, "Not bad enough."

As a younger man, Coach was known for ripping players' helmets off in practice and punching players on the school bus after a loss. Thus, he usually fielded small squads of maybe thirty-five players. Still, his players and their parents loved him. He meant well. He loved his kids, and he'd given his life to Hayes High School and the surrounding community of Avondale in Birmingham. Coach was respected like the high school principal, the local minister, and the one doctor. Coach Whitlark turned boys into men.

In the days of segregated Birmingham football, the high school teams belonged to the neighborhoods. Students walked or took city buses marked "specials" that transported them directly to school. The working class, public housing neighborhoods of Avondale, Kingston, and Woodlawn supported Hayes High.

On the night of the school's biggest victory in the last three years, the one that snapped a thirty-two-game losing streak, the residents of the housing projects flowed out of their homes to greet the school bus as it made its way back to the school. Kids, parents, and well-wishers ran screaming into the streets racing behind the bus. Coach Whitlark bragged, "It was like a scene on television, something out of South Africa."

Whitlark had put a few players in black colleges, the only option open to them. He even had one who made it all the way to the NFL as a special teams player for the Philadelphia Eagles. But most of Coach Whitlark's boys were from the neighborhood and high school was about as far as athletics was going to take them. Coach felt his job was to make them men, get as many as he could into college, and win a few games.

At his twentieth anniversary celebration at Hayes High School, three hundred former players showed up to honor Coach Whitlark. They witnessed something that night they'd never seen before: Coach cried.

Now, Coach looked across the field at Danny, and he saw the future. A future he would not be a part of. He was a dinosaur. Used. Damaged. The new way would never accept him. He was a segregation coach in what would soon be an integrated world. Still, he looked at Danny with pride. Coach had done his part. He'd been a link in the chain. He'd been a bridge to Danny's future.

After integration, the big white football colleges looked for "good blacks," the ones who could navigate the football field and the new society called integration. Danny stepped to the front of the line.

Danny became "The First."

Danny's presence inspired Coach's players. They looked at Danny and dared to dream. If Danny could do it, so could they.

Danny ran a few pass routes with the high school quarterbacks and receivers. He did it as much for the younger players as he did to keep himself sharp and razor tuned. He knew when he made a new move or a quick adjustment on a route the younger receivers would try it also. *Good*, he thought. He could teach without being overbearing. Danny didn't want anyone to feel he was above them.

Several older boys mingled along the sidelines. In their day, they'd played for Coach too. Jimmy Floyd, a fat wino, had been the fastest boy in the city at the one-hundred-yard dash. He'd won the State meet. A Gale Sayers on the football field, his exploits had occurred on segregated fields. "You came along too early," Coach Whitlark told him.

"There ought to have never been a time called too early," Jimmy spit back.

In Jimmy's day, the mid-1960s, the larger white universities in the Deep South would not touch a black player, even one with the talent of Jimmy Floyd. Yes, Jimmy could run the ball, but could he maneuver the slippery field of racism that led to the goal line of integration? Jimmy couldn't. He drifted off to tiny Miles College in Birmingham, got discouraged, and quit to hang out on the street corner. Now he was one of those guys who "could have been."

The 1970s had brought about a new era. The white colleges, tired of getting their butts kicked by the Nebraskas and Southern Californias of the world, turned to their own backyards and began recruiting black players. But the first players had to be the "right ones at the right time"—pioneers. Players who would set the benchmark, make blacks proud, smooth the white guilt over segregation, and wouldn't fight back.

The wonder boy of his neighborhood, Danny was a helluva athlete, who came from an intact family. He had integrated his Catholic school. He was smart and would not embarrass a university by flunking out. On the field, he was a game changer. A coach could see his own future in Danny; with an athlete like Danny, a coach could make himself a career.

It began for Danny the first time he scored at his high school. The local newspapers hailed it as the first time a black player had scored against a white high school. The papers called it history. Under the heading, "The First," the newspaper splashed Danny's picture as he crossed the goal line. From then on being The First was his calling.

The first time Danny ran onto the field at his college, thousands of fans stood and applauded. When he scored in his first game, the very first time he touched the ball, the stands erupted. Signs sprouted in the stands, "We love Danny." "Danny's our boy."

He was a hit, a role model. Many more could now follow. Kids all across the South could dream of playing football at their state universities. They no longer had to go up North or out West. They were no longer relegated to the minor league of Black college ball. Parents could encourage their kids to look up to Danny. Older black folks in his neighborhood held their heads up with pride. When Danny was interviewed on television news and asked why he'd chosen to be The First he responded, "I did it for the old folks." *What a young man*, everyone thought. Danny became the pride of the State of Alabama.

The integration of major college football in the State of Alabama had gone smoothly.

Or had it?

What they didn't know, what Danny didn't talk about with anybody, not even Coach Whitlark, was how unhappy it all made him.

It had been a calling for him, being The First. Now, it had become his job. When he woke up and started his day, he began it as The First. He would end that day as The First and all in between he was The First.

His every move was scrutinized, his every word analyzed. Afraid to make a mistake that could derail the entire process, he stayed close to his dorm. He had no social life. He had no one like Coach Whitlark. No one he could confide in. No one he could be honest with. No mentor. No friend.

Why couldn't he just play and have fun like the rest of the guys? Why couldn't he just be one of the guys? What would that be like? He couldn't tell people how much he felt like a piece of meat, a novelty, or a new pet when fellow students came up to him to feel his biceps or ask, "Can I feel your hair?" He never told anyone about the late night phone calls, when fans who had praised him in the daylight unleashed their venom on him after a night of drinking. "Nigger, you're dead." He didn't tell his parents how his teammates reacted with venom when they played a team with black players. He covered his ears, to drown out the noise of "Nigger, Nigger, Nigger," from his own teammates.

He never talked about how the normal became the abnormal for him. A beer in his hand at a party became a lecture from his college coach. The spotlight shone, and it shone brightly.

Who could he date? When a white classmate, Becky Sue, befriended him, Danny was scolded by his coach and reminded, "We don't mix colors here." No one asked what he did after games, when he sat in the television room, while his teammates partied. Being The First was lonely and isolated. But he couldn't say that. He couldn't behave like that. He couldn't lash out or have a man-to-man with his coach. He was The First, and that's just the way it was.

He had to play, play well, graduate, and shut up.

He was on schedule to graduate. On the field, he was magic in motion, racking up touchdowns with regularity. There was a freedom in playing the game.

A fall Saturday, the crisp air, cheering fans, in the huddle with his teammates, and his play being called, those things made him happy. That was fun! That made him forget that it wasn't about him.

Coach had told him, "It not about you. You're making a difference."

Sometimes Danny wished it were about him. Just once, that would be okay. Just once.

Coach Whitlark called. "Danny, I'd like you to talk to the boys at the end of practice. Tell them what it takes to make it. You're a great role model for them." Danny put on his smile, the one he hid behind when he became The First. "Sure, Coach," he answered.

Sisters

Tiffany ducked, feinted, and dribbled to her left. Tracey, thrown off balance, shifted her size nine feet and hustled to catch up. Tiffany, with a quick little quirky move, pulled up, quick-jumped and shot a laser that popped the net as the ball whipped through.

"Nineteen," Tiffany grunted, sweat soaking her jersey.

"Yeah," Tracey mumbled under her breath.

Tracey retrieved the ball. They didn't make eye contact. The pressure built. Tiffany felt it. Tracey felt it. Tiffany checked the ball. Tracey positioned herself at the top of the key.

Tiffany called out the score. "19-18."

"I know the score," Tracey shot back.

"Just letting you know, girlfriend." Tiffany barked.

"Right," Tracey mumbled.

The first one to twenty would win.

Both women were soaking wet on the hot, outdoor asphalt court. It was the dog days of an Alabama August, hot with no wind or shade. Tracey's shirt stuck to her abs. Tiffany, lean and wiry, wiped the sweat from her brow. She took her defensive stance.

Without hesitation, Tracey rose on thick, curving, muscular legs and let go a picture perfect jump shot. "Automatic," she boasted as she let it go. It snapped the net, 19-19!

"Deuce!" Tracey declared.

The three game series was tied at one game each. Both games had gone to the wire. First one to twenty in the third game would win the day's championship. Neither woman wanted to lose to the other. Best friends didn't count when it came to hoops.

They'd been competing since they met.

. . .

Tiffany, twenty-seven, was the sharpshooter. She was 5'8", a lean, pretty, blonde woman who could have been a model as easily as a basketball player.

Tracey, twenty-five, was the athlete, 5'9", thick, and well-conditioned. On the court, she made things happen through willpower and never giving up. Off the court, she was a sultry black diva.

They'd met in college.

Tiffany was a walk-on on the basketball team. She was a good player, not a great player, but she didn't need basketball for validation or to pay her way through school. She was not looking to play professional basketball, nor was she looking for a lifelong career after college. Tiffany played hoops because it was fun. She enjoyed it.

Tiffany came from money, so by walking on and giving the team valuable minutes off the bench, she saved a scholarship and thus became more valuable to the team and coach.

Tiffany was also headstrong.

She defied her father's choice of college, the University of Alabama, and instead chose their archrival Auburn University. She further infuriated her dad by majoring in education with the intention of teaching and coaching. Her dad, who had inherited his money, had Tiffany's life planned, down to whom she would marry and when. He also wanted her to get a law degree; something he had not done in his day.

"Trey got it all worked out," the women would laugh when they discussed Tiffany's life with her dad.

Tracey had come to the basketball team as a highly recruited athlete. Her brother before her had been a great athlete. Tracey did need the money and did want to play professional basketball. But Tracey had a plan for her life as well. She wanted to practice indigent law, "level the playing field." Playing pro ball for a few years would give her the money for a good start.

At the meal after her first practice in college, Tracey sat alone until Tiffany joined her. They bonded. Before long, whenever they were together they were laughing, giggling, and making fun of their teammates. It was not shocking to them how relaxed and trusting they were with each other. They loved spending time with each other. How they could be both silly and vulnerable with each other.

Rumors circulated that they were lesbians. They were not.

They became best friends, rooming together, sometimes even sleeping in the same bed together. They joked that they were sisters from different mothers.

They clicked. They didn't compete with each other on looks, getting the coach's attention, grades, or men. There were no cat and mouse games between them. They turned the stale, proper, drunken, Greek social life on campus on its head. They often dated the same guys, letting them think they were in control. They dressed in each other's clothes. They made the dean's list every semester. They were roommates on the road, visiting museums, and out of the way shopping locales. They took trips to New York and New Orleans. In short, they had a ball.

After graduation, Tiffany stayed around for a couple of more years of school to get her Master's and hang out with Tracey.

Tiffany taught and coached the girls' basketball team at the White Knights Christian Academy in the suburbs. It was a labor of love. "Sorry-ass girls," she would confide in Tracey. "Pussies. Wouldn't bust a grape." Still, Tiffany enjoyed the teaching. She wanted to do something besides make money. She wanted to "make a contribution." She figured she'd marry soon enough and once she had babies she would no longer work. Her steady, Bill, worked at the bank where her dad was a big shareholder.

. . .

After her graduation, Tracey made it across the pond to play ball in Russia. She became a top baller, banking $100,000 a year tax-free for the six months she worked abroad. Her plan was to play one more year before moving back to the States and beginning her law school journey. Then she ripped her knee ligaments into shreds. That had been a year ago. She was working her way back into condition with Tiffany who, as always, was there for her.

Tracey's boyfriend played pro ball in Italy. She loved him and would one day marry him, but the little-lady-sitting-around-waiting- at-home scene didn't work with her. She dated when she wanted and whom she wanted, with Tiffany often hooking her up with cute boys at the bank where Tiffany's boyfriend, Bill, worked.

They double dated and were very good at keeping "girlfriend" secrets. However athletic they considered themselves, they also loved dressing up and "being girlish," going out on the town to see how many heads they could turn.

During those days of summer, the women rode bikes, played tennis, and roamed the city looking for an outdoor game of basketball. Their passion was to ride up on a game of hoops with teenaged boys who could jump through the roof, but didn't yet possess the sound fundamental skills of the game. The girls, intelligent and in their athletic prime, would pull over, park their bikes and administer a butt whipping.

"Wanna school them?" Tracey would ask in front of the young teens, who would become so sufficiently disrespected that they would want to settle the "Who was better?" question right then and there. Grabbing the "thing" in their pants, the young boys would boast about what they would do to the "girls."

"Shaking my head on that," Tracy would laugh.

"If I thought you could handle me, I might let you," Tiffany would tease the teen boys.

"Let's ball," Tiffany would proclaim.

The game was on.

Tiffany, a laser long-shooter, played on the perimeter. Tracey's favorite line about Tiffany's shooting prowess was, "She can shoot it from the bathroom." Tiffany stretched the teenagers' defense, while Tracey used her athleticism and daring to steal loose balls, play rugged defense, and rebound.

The male teens on the outdoor courts could fly like kites, but there was a reason they were not playing organized ball, and Tracey and Tiffany exploited those reasons. Tiffany, already coaching, and Tracey playing at the women's highest level, knew how to win. They loved winning, especially beating boys. It had been a while since they'd lost in a scrap-up game.

"Don't let these girls beat you," they would taunt the boys.

"Spanking that bootie," they would laugh.

Today, they had visited their three favored courts, and they hadn't been able to get a decent game.

So it came down to one-on-one.

. . .

"Ready?" Tiffany asked. Sweat beads ran off her forehead, down her torso and off her legs. She dried her forehead on her T-shirt, exposing her pale flat stomach.

"Yeah," Tracey pushed through her lips.

Tiffany wanted to end it. She knew Tracey. Tracey got stronger the longer she played. She would never give up. Tracey had grown up playing against her brother, who was playing pro football. Tracey liked to get physical. *Just got to get off my jumper*, Tiffany thought.

Tracey gave Tiffany the hand slap on the last point. She broke down into her defensive stance, her long short pants nearly dragging the ground.

"It's on you, Tracey," Tiffany announced. "What's this one for? All the men or all the money?"

"I believe I won last time and took all the money," answered Tracey.

"Since we are remembering, I skunked you in horse that same day and took the money back," Tiffany reminded Tracey.

"Get the money," Tracey began. Tiffany joined in, "And you can get the men." They laughed.

"All the money," Tracey reassured her friend.

"All the money it is," Tiffany joined in.

The pounding of the ball on the concrete, the hunched forms of the two competitors amid the setting sun created an urban sports mural.

Tiffany dribbled forward then stepped back, cocked her right arm, and fired. Tracey leaped, arching her body to block the shot as the ball left Tiffany's hand. Tracey missed the ball and turned quickly to follow its arc. She slid her ass into Tiffany to pin her at the spot, stopping her from pursuing any errant rebound.

The rotating ball was only off by fractions of an inch as it rolled around the rim and finally rolled off, a miss.

"Damn!" Tiffany screamed.

Pissed, Tiffany growled.

"At least I got one," Tracey shot back.

"Your brother likes what I got," responded Tiffany.

"I know," answered Tracey.

Tracey's brother, Radio, not only liked Tiffany's ass, he loved Tiffany. They'd had an ongoing relationship for five years. They met one night when Radio had come to the college to visit his sister. He saw Tiffany, she saw him, and they had the most romantic weekend of their lives.

Later it had gotten complicated.

Trey, Tiffany's dad, wanted Tiffany to marry Bill the banker. Tiffany had resigned herself to that happening. She knew of her dad's history with his own father. He had resisted his dad's wishes for him to go to law school and to one day run the bank where Big Willis—her granddad—had worked. Tiffany saw how much her dad regretted disappointing his own dad, how much he drank to hide his pain.

Two years ago, Trey laid down the ultimatum. She had to stop seeing Radio, period. Trey insisted it was not because the young man was black; hell, after all, Trey considered himself a liberal. He wanted Tiffany to live the life he had planned for her and that life did not include Radio, who Trey actually liked.

She stopped seeing Radio, or at least told her dad she would. Tiffany and Radio agreed to tone it down. They kept things under cover. But, whenever Radio came to town from Los Angeles, they hung together like the lovers they were, with Tracey covering her girlfriend's tracks from Bill the banker.

In another time and place perhaps, Tiffany and Radio would have married, but neither had ever allowed the relationship to drift into those waters. Their love for each other was solid, and they were mature and realistic about it. They'd started as friends, moved into a sexual relationship; moved into a loving, sexual relationship; and moved into a best friends, loving, sexual relationship. They enjoyed each other's company, talking, and laughing. They had fun together and were silly together. But the relationship had caused problems for Tiffany and Radio loved her too much for that. He had been there for her when she had gotten into a fight with Trey and physically lost. She had been there for him when he'd been cut from the NFL and before he found refuge in Canada. Besides, Tracey and Tiffany were as close as Radio had ever seen two people. He did not want to come between his sister and her friend by making Tiffany choose.

When Tiffany promised her dad not to see Radio anymore she knew that was one promise she wouldn't keep. She kept it under wraps with the help of Tracey. She wondered if Trey knew that she still secretly dated Radio.

He did.

. . .

Tracey rushed to the basket. Tiffany wondered how she had missed. It felt good when it left her hand.

Tracey timed her jump, straining every muscle, but the rebound had Tiffany's name on it. The ball bounced long over Tracey's head, and Tiffany grabbed it like lost treasure. When Tracey turned, Tiffany had her feet set ready to launch.

"Damn!" Tracey screamed.

She broke to Tiffany and rose. She felt the rough leather bruising the tips of her fingers as she stretched to block the shot. Time stopped. Both women, in the setting sun, watched the ball bank off the orange square of the backboard, hit the front rim, hold on the rim for an eternal second, and then, roll off the rim.

"Foul," Tiffany barked.

"No way," returned Tracey.

They hustled to the loose ball.

Tracey came up with it.

"Time," she called.

Tiffany didn't mention the foul again. Neither did Tracey. You can't call a ticky-tacky foul on the game point.

"Ball should have gone," Tiffany thought.

They moved to opposite ends of the concrete court. Conserving energy, they did not talk. They didn't look at each other. Both stood. Neither wanted to give up an edge.

"I'm good," Tracey announced. "Let's do it," Tiffany agreed.

Tracey checked the ball. Tiffany set her feet.

Tiffany handed Tracey the ball.

Tiffany held out her hand. Tracey gave her some dap.

"Ready?" Tiffany asked.

Tracey nodded.

Tracey made a shimmy move with her ass and legs but did not move her feet. It looked as though she was taking off for a drive to the basket, but instead she held her position.

Tiffany momentarily went for the fake leaning toward the goal, but quickly regained her position. In that split second, was she too late?

"Game," Tracey declared. Tiffany countered, "No way." She sprang up for the block. Tracey let it go. Tiffany's fingers missed the ball. Off balance, she fell into Tracey. The girls, best friends, fell into a heap of legs and arms on the hard concrete court, their necks straining around one another to watch the ball arcing toward the goal. Was in a hit or a miss? Who cared!

They laughed. Then laughed louder and louder as the sun set behind the horizon.

Christmas Come Early

It was a grey overcast Sunday in late November when lanky and youthful Jim Mason moved his wife, two boys, and their belongings less than 200 feet directly across narrow 86th Street into old Mrs. Brown's three-bedroom red brick house, with a fenced back yard. "Buying makes more sense than renting," Jim told his wife.

Two months before to the date, elderly widow Bessie Brown, sporting her newly purchased $9.99 fire red wig, with matching purse and shoes, had gone next door to Mrs. Beulah Benson's house. "It's just not the same since Tom died," she told Beulah about living without her husband of fifty years. "I want to spend my last years on God's earth in Tennessee with my kin folks."

Before the "For Sale" sign could be firmly planted in the ground, Jim used his GI benefits and good paying job at the L&N Railroad to keep his family in the peaceful two-street community of Rosalind Heights. "Been here all my life," Jim declared of the Birmingham, Alabama neighborhood. "Why leave?" The deal left Mrs. Brown and Jim happy. The only remaining cog was Larry Brown.

Larry, Mrs. Brown's forty-five-year-old adopted son, hit the roof when he found out about the sale. "I will not leave my home," he swore to his mom. "This is the only home I've ever had. I'm not going back." Larry had spent the first seventeen years of his life as a ward of the state. He'd stayed in homes for unwanted children. He vowed he would never go back.

Angrier than his mom had ever seen him, Larry, slammed the door to his room, screaming, "How could you do this to me?" "Where am I going to go?" He wanted to know.

On the other side of his door, Mrs. Brown heard the sobs. Larry was crying. He'd never cried since coming to live with her and Tom. He had been a young man then. Wounded and wary, he didn't trust. It took Larry three years and lots of love to believe that Mr. and Mrs. Brown would not take him back to the state home for children. Now, twenty-eight years later, Mrs. Brown was taking his home away from him. He had taken it far harder than she could have imagined.

Mrs. Brown eased into Larry's room. Larry tried to stop crying. He gagged. He tried to control himself, but his body jerked and shook as he tried to manage his hurt, his anger, and his fear. He couldn't.

"You can buy the house. I'll sell it to you real cheap." Mrs. Brown pleaded, "I don't have any savings, or any pension. I need the money." It tore at Mrs. Brown's heart to hurt her son. "You can move with me to Tennessee," she begged.

Larry's body turned rigid, and his countenance changed. He reverted back to the young boy she'd first met, the boy who had never known love, the boy who was so afraid to love, so afraid of rejection.

Mrs. Brown reached out to comfort her son, but with an angry reflex, Larry slapped her so hard her old red wig flew across the room and landed in the hall. Mrs. Brown went flying into the wall. Larry, inconsolable, balled up in the corner, mumbling gibberish and crying hysterically like a child.

Mrs. Brown, terrified and bleeding from the mouth, stumbled from the house and headed next door to Beulah's. Larry had never raised his hand or voice to her. She didn't know this Larry. She was afraid. She gave Beulah the story and refused to go back into her home alone. Beulah called her nephew Roy. It would be at least two hours before Roy could get there from work. Beulah offered to call the police. Bessie begged off. No, she couldn't do that to Larry. No, they would have patience and wait. They did.

When Mrs. Brown saw Larry leave the house walking in a fitful hurry like a sullen child, she enlisted Beulah to help pack up her belongings. She got what she needed. "Ain't much I want," she told Beulah. She left the furniture, left her husband's old car. She didn't drive, and neither did Larry. She called her relatives in Tennessee and told them to come get her. It took them two days. There was no sign of Larry. Bessie said her goodbyes in the neighborhood. She left Larry a message telling him that he needed to move his belongings before Jim and his family moved in. And with that, Bessie Brown was gone from Rosalind Heights. She never saw her son again.

· · ·

Larry Brown...

No one in the Heights knew much about Larry. He was nondescript. A fair-skinned man with a closely cropped haircut, he always wore a dressy cap pulled over his eyes. He was neither handsome nor ugly. He was Larry. He worked at Sears downtown, and wore one of those grey custodial outfits with matching shirt and pants that had his name, "Larry," sewn in red thread over the shirt pocket. Larry was a common, everyday man. He'd never stand out in a crowd, except for his fast paced hip-switching walk. Larry switched his hips like a woman selling her goods on the street corner.

To the people in the Heights, Larry was always either going to or coming from the bus stop. He left home in the dark of morning and returned in the dark of night. He left going down one hill and returned coming up another. He refused to drive the rusted old 1966 white Ford his father left when he died, or any other car. He either walked where he wanted to go, or he would take the bus. Every now and then, at night, someone would drop Larry off at home, the driver never getting out of the car. Nosy neighbors never were able to get a good look at the driver. Was it a man or a woman? Larry would exit the car, offer brief hellos to the fellas under the streetlight, and hustle his fast walking, ass-shaking self on in the house. Larry would even show up in a cab every now and then. No one in the Heights ever traveled by cab. Who had the money?

But Larry was different. Larry didn't date. He had never been married. "When he walks, he switches just like a girl," Beulah and the older ladies in the neighborhood gossiped. Larry didn't hang out or talk and watch football with any of the men from the neighborhood. He didn't work on cars. He didn't do things men liked to do. The older women labeled him a sissy, meaning Larry's wires must be crossed, and he liked men instead of women.

. . .

I passed our old home and eased the shiny, brown 1971 Thunderbird with the half vinyl top down the tiny slope into Jim's driveway. It was my annual pilgrimage to the old neighborhood, something I always looked forward to. I'd already visited what neighbors were left, saving Mrs. Beulah, my second mom, and Jim, my old neighbor, for last. I would spend more time with them.

The neighborhood had changed. Something had been lost. The goodness and concern that had been inherent there had gone. It left with the many of us who had moved on and out. There was meanness in the air that had not existed and less concern for the upkeep of the homes.

I visited the people I had known and didn't bother to learn or know the new folks.

The rented house was empty. Jim had moved or was still moving. Jim's parents lived on the corner, meaning Jim had spent nearly his whole life between the three houses on this corner. I kicked on the emergency brake and threw the gear stick into park. Jim's new house was directly across the street.

The grey sky, pregnant with the rain to come, couldn't dampen my spirits. I was in the old neighborhood, and it felt good.

"My man." Jim poked his head through the door. Six-foot-six inches tall, he ducked beneath the door trestle, kicked aside a couple of boxes and with that big wide grin on his deep chocolate face, greeted me with a soul handshake. "Pull up a box or something and sit down." I negotiated the cluttered carport full of both Jim's and Mrs. Brown's furniture. I sat on a box marked "Ivory Liquid."

"I didn't realize you were moving today, man," I offered.

"Yeah, I got most of the stuff in yesterday," he said proudly. "Wasn't a bad move, just walking stuff across the street," he laughed.

I laughed. We slapped skin.

Jim fidgeted. He had been nervous ever since he got back from 'Nam. He blinked his eyes constantly. He blinked to a rhythm only he could hear. A word and two blinks, a word and two blinks, he repeated over and over. Jim smoked way too much weed; he repeated himself often and doodled with his guitar, fancying himself a six-foot-six inch Jimi Hendrix, wearing his hair like the rock legend. He had the luxury of flexible work shifts at the L&N railroad, working double shifts three days a week so he could be off the next three days.

"Dig it, man," Jim said behind red eyes. "May be some shit going down here today."

"What's up?" I quizzed, not wanting any trouble.

"Larry," Jim answered.

"Larry," I echoed. "Larry never bothered anybody."

"Damn fool won't come and get his belongings, man!" Jim blurted out. He blinked in rapid-fire order. "It's all lying in there on the floor—clothes, stereos, albums, a thousand pens, radios, and watches."

Jim's voice rose. "Larry's got women's clothes in there." Tears of laughter welled up in his eyes. Jim laughed, hard. "Panties, bras, all kinds of shit, man," he said, trying to quell his laughter. He held his big black hand out. I held mine out, and he slapped me some skin. "Larry's been dressing up in women's clothes. It's all piled in there in the middle of the living room floor." He pointed inside the house.

I looked at Jim in jest. He looked back in seriousness. "I'm not jiving, man." He stood. "Not jiving. Come on in, if you can get in."

Jim pulled open the screen door, and I could see his mom and pop in the living room on a scavenger hunt digging through what I assumed were Larry's belongings. I paid my respects. Old Mr. Williams, who lived in nearby Zion City was digging through Larry Brown's personal things as well. *What were they looking for? I wondered.* Jim stepped over a box in the doorway, spread his hands, and gestured, "See, what did I tell you?"

The pile of stuff was astonishing: Ladies dresses, hats, shoes, lots of women's undergarments, men's shoes, pants, shirts, stereos, ink pens, watches, albums, cigarette lighters, and what Jim called "some voodoo roots." Most of it lay unpacked on the floor. Jim's parents and Mr. Williams sorted and searched through the pile. "Let's go into the back, man." Jim motioned toward the hall. "I've got something to show you." Jim's mom shot him a look I couldn't decipher. She mumbled an inaudible grunt I couldn't hear under her breath. We stepped over several boxes leading to the rear of the house. I was starting to get a funny feeling that maybe I shouldn't be here. Mrs. Mason, Jim's father and Mr. Williams continued their search.

Jim led me through the maze of boxes, bags, and loose whatnot in the hall and into another equally cluttered room, a bedroom. Jim shut the door. We sat on two boxes.

"Larry left all this stuff?" I asked.

"Ever since Mrs. Brown left. I called his job three times asking him to come out and get it, and he keeps saying he's coming but he doesn't show," Jim countered. "He got pissed. Told me he'd get it when he was ready. I said, 'But Larry, it's my house.' He hung up on me. Hung up." Jim's eyes blinked away.

Jim reached for a small cedar box laying near a pile of old newspapers. I knew what would happen next. Jim's long charcoal-colored fingers, with manicured nails meticulously rolled a fat joint. "I've been asking myself what kind of man would leave his belongings in someone else's house for three days." Jim grinned. He blinked and waited for me to react. I didn't. "You know, legally anything here is supposed to be mine. Legally." He waited on my reaction again. I hid what I was really thinking. Jim reached into the box for a lighter and fired the joint up. The first wave of smoke exited through his nose. He took another hit, this one heavier and deeper than the first. It sent Jim into a whooping cough, but his eyes stopped blinking. Smoke raced from Jim's nose and mouth. His now not-blinking eyes turned an evening sun red. Jim handed the profusely burning illicit cigarette to me. Feeling uncomfortable, I begged off.

Jim hit the joint again. He leaned his head back and inhaled deeply. This time he let the smoke shoot from his mouth and nose like a train engine. It must have been some good shit, because Jim's mood lightened instantly. Euphoria set in. He stopped blinking, then whispered, "That fool left some money here." Jim leaned closer, "Hey, man, he left a lot of money."

Now things were becoming clear to me.

Jim gave me a "No shit," look.

"I'm talking about $5,000 in bills," Jim went on. "There's about $1,500 in change, all in quarters and dimes. There's $7,000-$8,000 in checks he's never cashed, savings bonds in the thousands."

I knew Larry Brown about like everyone else in Rosalind Heights. He was a mystery. But I could imagine if the dude showed up and his cash and belongings were missing and all picked over he'd be pissed.

"Why do you think my family is not here?" Jim answered, reading my thoughts. "Huh?"

The day was turning dark, the sun playing peek-a-boo with the clouds. Jim paused and looked out of the window. Thunder rumbled in the distance. The smell of rain filled the air. It wouldn't be long.

Jim peeked down the hall. His parents were turning Larry's stuff inside out. "We think there's more money here," he started up again. "I want him to come and get his stuff. I don't want any trouble, but…" Jim lifted up his jacket to show me the handle of a .38 Special resting comfortably inside his pants.

I sprang from my box seat.

"Give him his stuff," I said to Jim. "Let him go."

Jim's face twisted, a sign of uncertainty. "Yeah," Jim laughed. "Everybody keeps telling me, them sissies will kick your ass." He laughed louder. "That's funny ain't it? A sissy kicking my ass."

Silence. Jim sat thinking. "I think Mrs. Brown and those two guys who came here to move her got most of Larry's money."

More silence. Neither Jim nor I believed that.

Jim debated himself. "But I tell you, I sure could use some of it. Hell, I'm broke from the move. But, I just don't know. I've never taken anything from anybody before. But legally it is my house. So whatever is here is mine. Huh? Legally, I mean."

There was more silence.

Jim ended his own debate. "Maybe he'll come today."

We stood in the cluttered room alone in our jumbled thoughts. A loose thought raced from Jim's brain to his mouth before he could control it. "He better come on if he wants it all." He started to blink again.

I needed to leave.

We reentered the living room. Mrs. Mason and the two old men were still furiously searching. Mr. Mason reached down into an old denim jacket pocket and pulled out a wad of dollar bills enclosed in a rubber band. The others did not see him. I pretended to look out the window. Mr. Mason, who had retired on a meager pension from the city, stuffed the money into his own pocket. I did not want to be around when, and if, Larry Brown showed up.

Jim led me through the kitchen toward the side door. He pointed to several bags of coins, a full moneybox, envelopes full of cash and nearly a hundred savings bonds all on the kitchen counter. "That's the money, man."

I glanced at the loot and made my way to the door.

I wished Jim luck in his dealings with Larry. Jim grinned and slapped my hand. "Everything gonna be alright," he said. He repeated, "Gonna be alright."

The rain started.

Before leaving The Heights, I went next door to visit Mrs. Beulah. Mrs. Beulah, with no children of her own, had been the community mom. I could never visit the old neighborhood without seeing her.

Mrs. Beulah was in her usual post by the window. From the window, she commanded a view of every direction in the neighborhood. She saw everyone coming and going. I had not seen Mrs. Beulah in a year but she looked good, with her graying hair surrounding her sixty-five-year-old lineless round face. She gave me a huge hug.

We talked while seated in Mrs. Beulah's plastic-covered living room with pictures everywhere of her now dead husband. Through the window she continued to monitor the activities next door. When Jim Mason walked out of his house with a bag in his hands heading in the direction of his parents' house, Beulah jumped up and summoned me to the window. She pointed to Jim with the bag cradled between both hands moving swiftly across the street in the rain. I recognized the bag as the moneybag Jim had shown me on the kitchen counter. Mrs. Beulah never looked away from the window when she said to me, "I sure hope he doesn't keep that boy's money."

I tried to reassure her for the both of us. "No, ma'am, I'm sure he won't."

Lightning crackled across the sky followed by loud rumbling thunder. The rain poured.

A gray Chevelle Malibu rounded the corner. The car passed Jim on his way back across the street. The car screeched to a halt in front of Jim's new house and backed into Jim's driveway. A brown-skinned husky woman with a blonde wig perched atop her head got out of the driver's side. The rain poured over her. She pulled out a women's plastic hair covering and tied it around her head, preserving her wig. Larry Brown sat on the passenger side of the car. The woman opened the trunk.

Larry Brown was with a woman! I knew instantly the news of Larry Brown showing up to get his belongings with a woman was passing through the neighborhood like a lightning-fast telegraph line.

Larry Brown emerged from the passenger side of the car in his grey uniform. Mrs. Beulah gave me a well-intentioned punch in the ribs and motioned for us to go outside under the covered front porch. The two green metal outdoor chairs on her front porch were strategically located behind two tall overgrown shrubberies. Mrs. Beulah and I sat, she taking the chair with the most advantageous view of Larry Brown.

Larry wore a brown cap pulled way down on his forehead. His eyes darted, taking in all the immediate surroundings. The now pouring rain didn't bother him. He had things on his mind. He looked at the house that had been his home for the better part of his life. Then he turned towards Jim Mason.

Larry switched his hips toward Jim. The two men talked. They made no effort to get out of the rain. Jim stood 6" taller than Larry, thus Larry was constantly looking up, Jim looking down. Larry did most of the talking. We couldn't hear them. Jim used his hands to emphasize that whatever Larry was saying was wrong. The blonde began moving Larry's goods from the house. She silently dumped them carelessly into the trunk of the Malibu. The blonde then whispered something in Larry's ear. Larry went to the trunk of the car and removed several jackets and coats, including the denim jacket I had seen Mr. Mason with earlier. Larry thoroughly searched the pockets. The clothes did not yield whatever it was Larry was looking for. Concern registered on Larry's face.

Jim entered the house and returned with the green moneybox and the moneybags with the change. He handed it over to Larry. Larry fumbled with the top then wrenched the box open. His hands waded through the box as his eyes carefully searched each document and dollar. Larry's look screamed, "All the money is not here!" and turned to vengeance. He stood defiant in the rain. In a loud voice, he asked, "Where is the rest of my money?"

Lightning hissed in the distance. Thunder followed. Jim faked coolness but it was not a good fake. He was blinking out of control. "Hey, man, that's all I saw," came his answer. "All I saw," he repeated nervously. Blink. Blink. Blink-blink.

The men squared off like a noon shootout in the old west. No one moved. Rain poured. Time stood still. Like two angry street dogs, neither man made the slightest move, recognizing a twitch could set the other off. Mrs. Beulah did not breathe behind the bush.

I thought about my own escape. I would have to cross the street to get to my car.

Not now.

Larry threw the moneybox roughly on the front seat of the car. He stormed back into the house brushing past Jim Mason, knocking him off balance. Jim's reflexes took his hand to the .38 tucked in his pants, but he thought better of it.

"Oh! I knew it, I knew it," Mrs. Beulah whispered excitedly to me. "I knew he was gonna keep some of it. I just knew it. Wait till I tell Willa Mae." She then jumped up so fast the metal chair rocked back and forth, leaving a clacking sound. I heard her lift the phone from the receiver and begin dialing.

Before long, the diligent, but now wet-headed blonde had loaded the trunk and the back seat of the car with the various items that had been piled up on the living room floor. Larry had not been much help. Every piece of clothing or box the blonde brought out, Larry searched frantically. He retrieved his savings bonds, uncashed checks and coins, but the several thousand more in paper money was not there.

The blonde finished and sat in the driver's seat, disgusted with the whole affair. Larry made one final check through his belongings then confronted Jim again. On cue, Mrs. Beulah returned from her telephone conversation. It was a safe bet she would update her story for her audience later.

The blonde came up with a set of jumper cables and hooked them onto the running Chevelle and the old Ford. After three tries she got the Ford to start. Who was going to drive it?

Larry and Jim stood in an isolated corner of the yard, rain pouring over both men. As before, Larry did all the talking, and he was doing it about six inches away from Jim's face. Again, we could not hear. Larry's hands were inside the khaki pants he wore. Jim's hands wagged continuously in front of his chest, stressing another negative to whatever Larry was asking him. Larry stiffened. He removed his hands from his pockets. They were clenched in tight fists at his sides. Jim backed up a step. Mrs. Beulah grabbed my arm.

Larry hollered an inaudible sound and fiercely kicked the ground, uprooting a fine piece of freshly planted Bermuda grass. Before the grass had settled some five feet away, Larry Brown's right hand sprang towards Jim's chocolate face. Larry's index finger braked just short of Jim's nose. Larry's mouth moved in a slow deliberate manner. Jim Mason moved back a step. He placed his hand on the quiet, hidden .38 Special. Larry saw the gun. His mouth stopped moving. He got the message.

Silence.

Thunder roared.

Their eyes spoke the next few sentences. Larry's eyes sent out a warning. Jim's eyes accepted the threat. Larry Brown moved a step closer and spat down by Jim Mason's size 14 feet, missing them. Larry called out, "You dope head!" Jim countered, "You sissy!" Larry walked off toward the car. It was not the walk of the old, hip switching Larry, but more deliberate, defiant, and forceful. Larry turned one last time to Jim Mason. He spat on the driveway. The blonde pulled the Chevelle out onto the street.

Larry got into his dad's old car, which was still running. No one in the Heights had ever seen Larry drive before. Larry shifted into gear and was gone!

Mrs. Beulah headed for the waiting phone.

The rain stopped. The sun, back on the scene, began its daily descent. I started across Jim's yard toward my car. The streets were empty. Most of the porches were clear, more than likely the phones were not. I backed my car out of the driveway. Jim Mason, on the lookout, walked out to my car and leaned through the driver's window. There was enough sunlight for me to see a man-in-the-moon smile plastered all over Jim's face. I lowered my gear stick into drive. Jim grinned in my direction. For the first time, I felt awkward in the old neighborhood. I was ready to leave, maybe never come back.

"Well, my man, he's come and gone." Jim laughed, blinking his eyes. Blink. Blink. Blink-blink. My car continued to roll. I did not want to stop. Jim laughed louder. Blink-blink. The car rolled past my old house. Jim's laugh followed. I wondered if he still had the pistol on him. The last thing I heard Jim say was, "Christmas come early this year."

Mr. Braswell

Every time they told the story, and it seemed they found a reason to tell it every time they got together, even now more than forty years later, in the year 2013, they would laugh their asses off. The laughs were deep, gut-wrenching laughs that gave credence to the absurdity and sadness underneath the surface of the situation.

It was all so long ago, another lifetime, another century, in that dark hell of racism in Birmingham, Alabama as the segregated 1960s gave way to the integrated 1970s.

There was the racism of the Ku Klux Klan, and violence and death in the 1960s. But there was also the racism of the 1970s and of Mr. Braswell, a man who wielded economic power and used it to practice the racism of humiliation.

. . .

"I know where you can find a job."

July Brackett, Mr. Know-It-All, was running off at the mouth big-time. July knew everything about anything, and every now and then he'd even be right about something.

He was at his best when holding court with the fellas, on the hill, under the streetlight on 86th Street in the Heights. His favorite topic, the one he loved to talk about more than any other, was July. "July is my favorite month of the year," he loved to say. "I love me some July."

Everyone knew that. There wasn't a mirror made that July could pass without taking another good long look at July. At twenty-five, he lived with his parents and his adult brother and sister. Every dime July earned as a maintenance supervisor at one of the local high schools he spent in black downtown Birmingham buying the latest men's fashion. July longed for integration, primarily so he could shop at the fine men's clothing stores in the white section of downtown.

July favored continental slacks, silk shirts, Florsheim shoes, and a French tam for his head. Slender and lean, July in another place and time might have been a pitchman for a clothing manufacturer, maybe even a model.

July had information Cool, Goose, and Radio wanted. They listened, all ears. But July enjoyed making them wait.

Finally.

"Go down to the City League," July instructed. "You know the City League, they like the Urban League. They have a listing on all kinds of jobs around town. The crackers got to hire black folks now 'cause of the civil rights laws and class action lawsuits. You know ain't no black folks working at these companies unless they janitors. You boys might get lucky," he told the younger boys.

In post-1964 Birmingham, the white private companies and Birmingham's major corporations ran the risk of violating new federal law and faced crippling economic boycotts if they did not hire black people in positions other than janitor. The companies were eager to fill their unwritten quotas and a good recommendation from The City League, the agency responsible for finding bright young blacks to take the jobs, would go a long way toward getting one hired.

"It's the nineteen seventies, baby." July primped as he talked. "Black folks finally gon' be free. Or at least be able to get a job."

With that, he gave his sidekick, Jim, some skin, laying it on him heavy and cool.

Jim Mason, six-foot-six, was Goose's older brother. He was quiet and made a great "under the streetlight" sidekick for the talkative July. He had been to fight "the gooks" in Vietnam and come back a different person.

The streetlight on the hill was the hanging place after dark. Summer nights after dinner, the fellas would gather under the light, crack jokes, and tell stories and lies until deep into the night. July, Jim, Shorty, and Rat, all twenty-five-years-old with full-time jobs, would school the younger boys who were all twenty-one.

"You boys educated," July continued. "Them crackers looking for you. They love sharp, young, educated Negroes, like y'all. Can't call y'all niggers no more."

In a rare moment in time, July ran out of things to say. He thought. You could see the wheels spinning inside his head, but nothing came out of his mouth. Everyone watched him. He paraded around. Still nothing. He couldn't prolong the inevitable any longer. He gave up the desired information.

"Okay. Downtown on Fourth Avenue, about 17th Street. It's in the same building as the Urban League, dark and dingy up in there. What that cracker name Jim that got the jobs?"

"Mr. Braswell," Jim mumbled, without looking up.

"Braswell, he got the jobs on a sheet of paper," July grinned. "Check it out. There's only one catch…"

. . .

"Fuck that peckerwood. He ain't rubbing up against me." Goose spit the words back at July in the glow of the streetlight. "Nah, Jack, fuck that shit."

July had just finished explaining "the one catch" the boys would face. July explained that Mr. Braswell was a pervert. July laid it out, "Mr. Braswell will interview you first, in a polite and professional manner. Once he says you qualified for one of his jobs he gon' pull out a list of jobs that you might interview for. Then he gon' show them to you."

Cool's interview with Mr. Braswell was the first scheduled. Cool had a two-year Associate's Degree and qualified for many of the sales positions the companies offered through the City League.

Radio met with Cool after his interview, and Cool confirmed what July had said. "Braswell…" after the interview Cool made a point of no longer addressing him as Mister. "He shut the door . . . " Cool began. "He pulls out the piece of paper then he comes around from behind the desk and stands over the desk and shows you the paper with you looking over his shoulder. He sticks his ass out like a woman, and he then rubs his ass up against your crotch. Grinding on your dick. And the bastard is grinning the whole time." "Oh shit!" Radio exclaimed.

"It made me sick," Cool confessed.

The silence between the boys spoke volumes.

Radio asked Cool. "Did you let him do it?"

"What you gon' do?" asked Goose. "Tell your mama and daddy? What they gon' do? Hell, that white man could probably get all our daddies fired."

"Man is there anything we can do?" Radio asked.

"The way they got this shit set up," Goose proclaimed, "If you poor and ain't got no connections, you got to go through Mr. Braswell to get to the jobs."

They all nodded in resignation.

"Did you get the job?" Radio asked.

"Yes. I got to meet the people over at Penny's tomorrow," Cool answered. "He sounds like I'll get hired."

"Is that it?" Radio asked, his mind searching for answers about his own interview. "Is that all he did?"

"Yeah, that's it," Cool relayed. "Sick old bastard. He barely touches you, but it's the thought. Then he goes and sits back in his chair behind the desk and just stares at you as if to say he wants more. He enjoys it."

"Wish there was somebody to tell," Radio said wistfully, knowing there wasn't.

"Who gon' take our word over that white man?" Goose demanded.

"White man say you lying, then you lying and everybody, including the police gon' back him," Goose rambled on angrily. "Find your ass sitting in jail, for insulting a white man. If it was white boys, his ass would be under the jail."

Goose continued, his anger flaring. "We ain't got no connections. Our folks don't know nobody. We can go get on the list for a plant job, but hell, they laying people off."

"He ain't touching me," Goose said. "I don't play that shit."

Two months later with no job prospects, Goose went for his interview.

True to his word Goose did not let Braswell rub against him.

Goose did not get a job. He was given a bad recommendation. Goose's negative recommendation beat him to every job interview he went to. He was labeled uncooperative, angry, a radical, and possibly a violent militant, the last guy a good respectable white company would hire. After all, The City League was a black agency. If he didn't have a good recommendation from The City League, then he had to be a bad apple. The personnel directors overlooked the fact that there could be any issue with Braswell, who was white. With no degree, no contacts, and the City League the main pipeline, Goose's options were limited.

Radio walked into the small office and sat in the cheap unstable chair in front of the desk Braswell sat behind. Braswell was polite, unlike the white men of the era who did not have to be. He was slight of build with a protruding stomach riding below his beltline. He wore black-framed glasses and a black thin tie that hooked onto his shirt collar. He talked about the City League, probed Radio's work interest, and even made a joke.

Radio's hope in addition to getting a job was for Braswell to stay behind the desk.

No way.

Braswell pulled out the clipboard with the list of jobs on it and came grinning around the corner of the desk. He closed the door, stood in front of Radio, and laid the clipboard with the jobs on it on the side of the desk. Braswell leaned over the clipboard. He made sure his body blocked the positions available and the companies that were doing the hiring. Radio would have to look over his shoulder to see the vital information. Radio, his mind racing, and his nose turned up in a sneer, remained seated.

"Stand over here, and you can see better," Braswell said. Radio hesitated and answered, "I can see it from here." Braswell moved the paper, so Radio could not see it.

Radio assessed his situation. He needed the job. He had a degree but no prospects, no skills other than football, and he would have to wait until next season to try out. This program run by the City League was put in place to help people with no contacts and no hope like him. Like his friend Fat and others he could go up north or out west and get a job, but hell, he didn't know anybody there. Where would he start? Cool had gone for his interview at Penney's and was already working. Radio hated this slimy, sick cracker.

Radio stood up. Braswell hid the paper wanting him to come closer. Radio took the step. He looked over Braswell's shoulder. Braswell moved backward into Radio. Radio moved back so Braswell could not touch him. Braswell covered up the paper with the list of names.

Neither spoke a word. They didn't have to.

Braswell uncovered the paper and moved backward again to touch Radio's crotch area. He rubbed himself against Radio's dick. Radio resigned himself and looked at the job choices Braswell offered. Braswell grinded his ass across Radio's dick. Radio chose a sales position to go for at the Xerox Corporation and moved away from Braswell.

Afterward, Radio puked in the parking lot.

Within two weeks, Radio was hired and went to work in the Xerox sales training program.

The Braswell incident was an eye opener for the guys who had grown up in a positive sheltered environment in Rosalind Heights. They'd never been preyed on before. It was their "Welcome to the World" moment.

. . .

Now all in their sixties and sitting at Green Acres chicken restaurant in what is described as new Downtown Birmingham, Cool, Radio, and Goose laugh about their upbringing. They talk about how lucky they were. They had grown up in homes with hard-working dads and loving moms. They played baseball and football in the street and rode their bikes everywhere. They built cabins in the woods and had a social club. They made friendships for life.

Inevitably, the talk always ends up back at Braswell.

"He had to humiliate us before he could give us the jobs," Radio commented.

They reminisce on July and his answer when they had asked him how he, Jim, and Shorty knew so much about Mr. Braswell. July had laughed and said, "We working, ain't we?"

Jim had responded, "Man, I went to Vietnam. I got a wife and two boys and a high school education, what choices do I have? All I learned in 'Nam was to smoke pot and hunt gooks."

A solemn moment overcomes the now-elderly men "I wonder if he is dead?" Goose asked. "Probably was a fucking Sunday school teacher."

They laugh uneasily.

Cool looked to Radio. Radio looked back at Cool. Goose did not catch the secret looks.

. . .

Weeks after his interview, Radio got up the nerve to ask Cool a burning question. He didn't want to know, but he had to know. "Did he wink at you?" he asked Cool.

Cool played it cool, "Did who wink?" he asked.

"You know what I'm talking about," Radio returned.

Cool dropped his head. "Yeah, Bastard looked at my crotch area and winked at me as I was walking out the door."

"Made me sick," Cool confessed.

They kept the confessions of the secret winks to themselves. The secret increased their anger.

They saw Braswell again. It was another of their secrets. Goose didn't know. Nobody knew. It was the one thing both men could have gone to jail for a long time for or even been killed.

After the confessions regarding the winks, Radio and Cool hatched a plan.

As darkness fell early one October evening, they hid in the parking lot by Braswell's car their faces covered with Halloween masks. Braswell walked into the trap. The boys surprised him. The first blow to Braswell's head sent him spinning to the ground. The level of the boys' anger surprised them. They beat Braswell down to the pavement with fists of anger. Braswell whimpered as the boys kicked him for good measure. Both boys cried as they hit and kicked Braswell. Blood flowed from Braswell's face. They left Braswell lying there crying and begging not to be hit anymore. "Don't you do what you did to anybody else," they warned him over the sobs. The boys ran for their lives.

They caught a bus to a different neighborhood and then walked home from there.

Daily, they feared the cops would come for them. A ring of the doorbell would send Radio to his room, afraid it was the Sheriff. A phone call would send a shiver of fear through Cool. One night while hanging under the streetlight, the Sheriff's car rolled through the Heights on a routine drive-through. Radio and Cool spotted the car and took off running for their secret camp in the woods.

They had a plan. They buried a can of money in the ground at the camp. If a getaway was needed, they would take buses to separate locations. Radio would go to British Columbia, Cool to Acapulco. They would hole up six months, then meet in Oakland, California and begin new lives.

No one ever came. Perhaps Radio's warning to Braswell saved them. "Tell anybody, and we will tell what you do to young boys and we'll kill you."

The boys would later send Don Charles from the neighborhood to apply for a job. He got a job with no problems. Braswell no longer came "from around the desk." He no longer violated the boys who came to see him. After the beating, Braswell conducted himself professionally, as he should have all along.

. . .

Stuck in the memory of yesteryear, the elderly Cool broke the silence. "Boy I'd love for somebody to try some shit like that today. At least today's kids can tell their parents. They got cell phones. Could take that bastard's picture. Today, at least, we could get his ass fired."

"Yeah," Goose replied. "Shit, look how many years I been looking for work. Somebody should have done something."

Radio and Cool's eyes met.

"Yeah," Cool agreed.

"Yeah," Radio said. "Somebody should have done something."

Fat In Town

Like a Black and White, B-Movie, big-bellied king, "Fat" — gold toothed, and 310 pounds — lay sprawled across the king-sized bed in his motel room on Airport Highway in Birmingham, Alabama. Maybe six feet tall, Fat, a brown-skinned Buddha, propped himself up on pillows, one hand tightly gripping a half-filled glass of Crown Royal.

"Shee-it. It's good to see you fellas," he breathed in a raspy voice. "I had to come see the fellas one more time."

It was 1988, and Fat had come home. Well, not exactly home. He no longer had a home in Birmingham. He'd given that up twenty years ago right out of high school when he moved to Los Angeles.

Grinning and half-drunk, Fat and his friend, "The Tin Man," had driven 2,200 miles from Los Angeles to Birmingham to see everybody. They occupied Room 39 at the Airport Highway Motel.

The fellas, Goose, Truck, Cool, and Radio, surrounded Fat's bed seated in cheap, worn motel chairs, grinning like willing subjects. It had taken each of them some time to get used to this broken-down version of Fat, raspy voice and all. This was not the Fat they remembered from growing up.

Fat, in town, brought the fellas together for an impromptu reunion. That hadn't happened often as adults. There was the occasional Bid Whist game, but families and job responsibilities meant less time today than yesterday.

When Fat called Truck with the news of his failing health and his impending trip to Birmingham, the fellas cleared their calendars. They had been "running dogs" in the old neighborhood of Rosalind Heights. Fat was the oldest, Cool a year younger, and the others a year younger than Cool.

Fat, thirty-seven, looked sixty-seven. The all-day daily dose of Crown Royal, greasy fried chicken with extra large fries, prescription pills, and life in South Central Los Angeles had taken its toll. A debilitating stroke meant Fat could no longer control the left side of his body. "It's dead to me," Fat lamented. The dozen pills he gobbled down daily were supposed to slow down his deterioration, but the alcohol sped it up instead.

Fat's doctor had not given him a death sentence, but how could he live like this? He swallowed pill after pill, downing them with Crown Royal.

"Shee-it! I still can take care of business with a woman," he volunteered, grabbing his crotch with his good right hand and squeezing. "That's what I'm saying." He laughed a hoarse, throaty laugh and held on to himself.

Fat grabbed the bottle on the bedside table and turned it up, the brown liquid disappearing into his mouth behind his gold tooth and down his throat. His once vibrant big brown eyes sparkled. He set the bottle back down, knocking over some of the vials of prescription pills. The fellas scrambled to pick up the loose pills.

Fat grabbed his crotch and took a deep, frustrated breath. "Got to pee," he said. It was Tin's job to get Fat in and out of the bathroom, but Tin had gone to visit some of his cousins in the projects. "But shee-it, I don't feel like trying to get over there." Fat held on to his penis through his pants.

He turned his attention to the fellas.

"Radio, I gave you that name. You was always talking, like a damn radio, wasn't he?" he motioned to the others.

"Yep." "Yeah." "Uh huh," came the chorus of Cool, Truck and Goose.

"With Radio, you could get any station at any time. Name a subject, and he had some info for you: a song, sports, news, politics, the war," Fat laughed. "He could talk a cat off of a fish truck."

Radio laughed. He liked the name Fat had given him.

"Yep, he was like Tall Paul," Goose reminded them." Remember Tall Paul, Fat?"

"Hell yeah," Fat instantly responded. "Tall Paul was the best disc jockey Birmingham ever had. Brother gave you the news, music, and gossip. Back in the day, black and white people followed Tall Paul. "TALL PAUL, Y'ALL!" He shouted as if on the radio.

"You supposed to be drinking like that?" Radio slipped the question in.

They had all wondered as Fat downed drink after drink.

Radio naturally would be the one to ask. He and Fat's relationship as teenagers had been close. As adults, they hadn't seen each other in the twenty years since Fats had left Birmingham in 1968.

Fat responded, "Doctor says take the medicine every day and don't drink. I told him, Shee-it, I'll make you a deal. I'll drink one day and take my medicine one day. Got to have my Crown."

Radio admonished him, "I'm sure the alcohol nullifies the pills."

"Radio," This time it was Fat's turn to change the subject. "You know what I remember about you?" he asked.

Radio shook his head, no.

"When we would ride our bikes to the store," he paused.

Radio interrupted. "You had that fast English bike your uncle got you."

"Okay, shut up now," Fat shot back. "I'm trying to say something."

"When we would go the store…" Fat tried to say more but stopped. Whatever he wanted to say meant a lot to him. The words caught in his throat and refused to come out. He averted his eyes. Tears welled up in his eyes. Pent up emotion almost bubbled over.

The fellas all looked away, pretended they didn't see. Fat was still the king, and none of them wanted to see him cry.

Fat fought through it.

Fat continued, "If you had a dime, you would give me a nickel." BOOM!

The words reverberated around the room. "If you had a dime you would give me a nickel." A solitary tear rolled out of Fat's eye. The fellas all understood. They knew Fat was talking about more than nickels and dimes.

Radio turned the attention back to Fat. It was Fat's day, Fat's weekend.

"Yeah," Radio chimed in. "And if you had money you would get a honey bun and a 16-ounce Nehi® strawberry soda. You loved those honey buns."

"Yeah," Fat grinned, patting his ample belly.

The five friends laughed. It felt good. They didn't want to think of that other stuff.

. . .

Growing up, Radio had been the star of the group. He made it to college on a football scholarship. He had been to the NFL and played in Canada. Now he was in television, doing news on the West Coast. Radio had been the game player. Name the game, baseball, football, basketball, running track in the street, and Radio played it, loved playing it, and played it well. There was one constant—Radio always had Fat on his team. When it came time to choose, Fat was always Radio's first round draft choice. "I got Fat," he would proclaim to no one's surprise.

Fat was a country boy, from Lowndes County, Alabama. He was big and burly, a good athlete, and could knock a fast-pitched rubber ball halfway down the hill with an old used broom handle. He showed up in the Heights one day at twelve years old. He just showed up. His family or at least the family he came to stay with already lived there.

Fat's dad drove over the hill in his Blue Fleetwood Cadillac one day and in the back seat he had Fat, his son, the one the fellas had never met. Fat moved in with his dad's family, five houses down from Radio. He lived with his father, stepmother, two half-brothers and later a half-sister and his dad's twin brother, all in a three-bedroom house.

Fat had relatives who lived on the other side of the hill from Radio. One uncle, Freddie, was single, and Fat would spend a lot of time as a teenager cutting his grass, washing his uncle's new Gran Prix Pontiac and occasionally "peeling rubber" driving it up and down the street.

Fat's uncles and dad were men's men. They had the truck stop arms and upper bodies of country boys used to heavy, hard labor. They all worked for the same meatpacking plant, Roscoe's Meats.

They all were deliverymen, driving trucks full of meat to groceries and supermarkets. Occasionally, one of the uncles would show up at home in his delivery truck with pounds of meat they'd helped themselves to at the company's expense. It was a fringe benefit of the job.

Fat's dad and uncles drove big shiny new cars: the Gran Prix, Cadillacs, and Buicks, and they drove them fast, flying up and down the hill as they went back and forth to work.

Fat's other uncle, Leontis, was married with two kids. His home became Fat's home away from home. Between his uncles and Radio's house and family, Fat found the family life he couldn't find in his new home.

On the surface, Fat's childhood looked as normal as his friends. At home in his dad's house however, Fat quickly became the outsider. His stepmother didn't want him there. A child vagabond, Fat spent as many hours outside the home as he could, leaving home early in the morning and returning home near bedtime. Fat spent his summer days with his Uncle's family, Radio's family, and any neighbor that would take him in for the day, feed him and give him a daily dose of love. There was always one stipulation. Fat had to go home at the end of the day, and he hated it.

When the fellas hung out under the streetlight in front of Radio's house, laughing, singing, and talking, Fat was always the last to leave. Only after everyone had gone home and the streetlight shone solely on him would Fat reluctantly head home.

Fat's high school graduation and a legendary whipping he put on his two stepbrothers finally pushed him over the edge.

No one in Fat's house came to his graduation. The moms on the hill who had become Fat's surrogate family all showed up. Radio's mom, Mrs. Betsy, from across the street and Fat's aunt attended. They bought him a suit to march in, gifts, and plenty of hugs and kisses. They also gave him the love he wanted desperately but could not find at home.

Fat was smart. He made good grades, but college was out of the picture without any money. The military represented Vietnam. "I already got enough trouble," Fat resigned to himself. Fat's dad gave him an ultimatum: "Leave." It hurt. His family didn't want him. The fellas knew how bad it hurt but never talked about it.

Fat left Birmingham shortly thereafter, heading to Los Angeles. Trying to hide his hurt, Fat bragged on getting out of the South. "I'm heading to LA, baby. Movie stars. Shee-it." Underneath it all, the fellas ached for him.

. . .

Throughout the day, old friends popped into the motel room. The word had spread that Fat was in town, and he wasn't in the best of health. Everyone from the hill in The Heights wanted to see him.

Within minutes of each other, both of his old girlfriends from the neighborhood had come to see him. As Marian entered the room, Brenda was leaving. They spoke to each other. They were cordial. Both were now married to other men. But they were still rivals for Fat.

Growing up, they had lived within eight houses of each other. They knew each other. They both knew that the other was in love with Fat. They had to. When Fat got his black '57 Chevy, with the glass packed mufflers that he had bought with his summer job in the steel plant, he would park it in front of Marian's house, and a couple of hours later, it would be parked outside of Brenda's. When leaving their respective homes, the loud mufflers would announce his departure as he shifted gears heading down the hill.

"Rap, rap, rap." There was a knock at the motel room door. In walked Fat's old nemesis.

Don Charles was taller and bigger than any of the fellas as boys. He was Fat's age, and he and Fat would often fist fight over ballgames, machismo, and Don Charles' envy of Radio. When choosing up for games, Don Charles was always on the other team.

"I ain't gon' fight your big ass no more," Fat grinned at Don Charles from his bed. The fellas laughed.

Don Charles announced, "I ain't here to fight neither." They all laughed.

Fat did not try to get up. His left side had him rooted to the mattress. Don Charles came over and gave Fat some dap.

Don Charles laughed, "Anyway, I could probably whip your broke-down ass now." Don Charles balled his fists.

"Probably," Fat laughed.

Shorty was next. Older than Fat by a couple of years, he had been more comfortable with Fat and the fellas than the guys his age. When the fellas were pre-teens, the parents on the hill had trusted Shorty with escorting them on the Saturday trips downtown for shopping and a movie. Shorty had multiple nicknames, with his family and neighbors calling him Shorty, and the fellas calling him "The Bionic Eye" because his eyes popped out of his head.

The joke was that The U.S. Government used him to spy on the Russians. He could see all the way to Moscow.

"So what the Russians up to?" Fat asked.

Shorty busted out in a good-natured laugh. His eyes darted to the bottle of Crown Royal. "Crown Royal, that's my favorite drink," he proclaimed.

Fat shot back, "Shee-it, you should have brought some." Fat did not give him any, and Shorty backed off.

"Still think you can sing like Smokey Robinson?" Goose asked Fat.

"Shee-it. What you think?" was Fat's raspy response. Goose and Fat had lived across from each other, but Goose was not athletic or tough enough for Fat. They were boys, but not tight. Goose had been closest to Truck.

"Yeah, we would all be hanging out there trying to sing, but no one could sing Smokey but you," Goose responded. Goose got up and sang the words to the hit, "The Tracks of My Tears." He demonstrated the dance moves of Smokey and the Miracles.

Fat smiled at the memory. He had been the strongest, the most handsome, a good student, and yes, he could sing.

Goose and Fat had gotten sideways once, and the issue wasn't about either Goose or Fat. Fat's cup boiled over, and he got into a serious fistfight with his two stepbrothers who at the time were 12 and 15. Fat was 16.

The two brothers, Randy and Michael, got all the benefits of family Fat never received. Fat didn't even look like them. They were fair-skinned and curly headed with "good" hair while he was more cocoa brown with the tight-balled hair of most blacks.

Michael, known as JuneBug, was the same age as Radio, Goose, and Truck. He was that guy no one wanted on their team for pickup football games. When he did play, because he was needed to make an even number of players, he was always the center. "You hike," would be his instruction in the huddle. No one worried about his self-esteem. He couldn't play. If you couldn't play, no one wanted you on his team.

The fight between Fat and his stepbrothers escalated from an argument during a game of foursquare in the street.

Michael accused Fat of "disrespecting our mom."

Fat let them know "Your mommy is not my mom. She has never treated me like a son."

"You ain't her son," Michael shot back. "You ain't nobody's son. Nobody wants you."

Knowing he had crossed the line, Michael grabbed his younger brother and took off running for the safety of home. But Fat, hurt and in a rage, caught up with Michael under the streetlight, threw him to the ground and started to pummel him unmercifully. With all his fury, and tears flowing, Fat rained down lefts and rights on Michael with a vengeance. Michael tried to fight back but he wasn't much of a fighter.

It was a massacre. Fat picked Michael up and slammed him back to the ground, taking out all his rage on his brother.

Maybe the fellas could have stopped him, maybe not. They'd all seen Fat fight before, but he was trying to hurt his stepbrother. All his resentment flowed from his fists.

Randy came back to help his brother. He jumped on Fat's back, but Fat reached up, grabbed a handful of Randy's curly hair, and flipped him on his back. He kicked him while he was down.

Fat beat their asses all over Radio's yard.

JuneBug jumped up and ran toward their house shouting, "Come on Randy, I'll tell Daddy on him."

Fat started to go after them, but Goose interceded. He pleaded, "Fat, Fat!" Goose blocked Fat's path. Fat almost took his rage out on Goose, but Truck held on to him. The brothers made it home. Lights clicked on in the living room of the house.

. . .

The Tin Man was back. "What's up, Tin?" Fat greeted him as he walked in the door.

As fat and sloppy as Fat had become in the twenty years since the fellas had seen him, the Tin Man was as thin as a rail. They were truly an odd couple. The Tin Man was close to 6'2" and soaking wet maybe weighed 170. Tin fell on the other bed, turned his back to the others, and tried to nod off.

"Tin brought me all the way cross-country. Wouldn't be here without Tin. Tell 'em, Tin."

Tin nodded toward the fellas. Tin's obvious loyalty to Fat, endeared him to the fellas. Tin rolled back over, to get his nap.

Fat continued. "Got a new hog for the trip. Did you see it out there?" Fat asked.

"The red one. I knew it was yours," Radio responded.

"Hey, baby, they got to see Fat coming," Fat bragged about his new Cadillac.

"I got me a nice settlement from the job," Fat volunteered. "Getting Disability, Social Security. When your body goes, they give you money."

The fellas, not knowing what to say, all nodded.

"Got me a family," he offered.

He paused. "I'm a better daddy than I ever had."

He bragged. "Tell them, Truck."

. . .

Truck, the color of shiny black coal was the darkest among the group and before Black became beautiful, he had always caught hell about it. Luckily in the mid-1970s, James Brown rescued Truck, and all Blacks, by making the number one record, "Say It Loud — I'm Black and I'm Proud." Black then became cool and Truck would say, "The blacker the berry, the sweeter the juice."

Also, Brenda, one of Fat's girlfriends, was Truck's sister. Fat and Truck were tight.

Truck was the only one of the group to have gone to California to visit Fat. Working at the Chicago Bridge and Iron Steel Plant, Truck drove a crane, made good money, bought a plane ticket, and made the long flight to California.

Truck reported back to the boys that Fat's life wasn't that much better in California than it had been in Alabama. Fat had stayed with an uncle on his birth mama's side of the family. The uncle was an abusive alcoholic. He and Fat had gotten into a scuffle, and Fat kicked his ass. The Uncle grabbed his gun, and got off a shot as Fat left the apartment running down the alley for his life. He never went back.

Fat slept in the coin-operated laundromat until he met Beulah and her two kids early one morning while she washed. Fat moved in and stayed until he got enough money to move. He gave Beulah his last paycheck as thanks and moved to Long Beach. He got a job in the shipyard, married, and fathered a couple of kids. Never having a family of his own, he wasn't the best at it. He drank, ate, and smoked himself into a stroke.

When Truck returned from California, he had some news the fellas had never heard.

"Fat talked about his life while I was out there," he said. The fellas had never heard Fat's life story before he showed up in the Heights at age twelve.

"As a child, Fat stayed with his birth mama until, for some reason he never knew, it was decided that he wouldn't stay there anymore. She didn't want him anymore, but no one told Fat. His daddy picked him up and took him to the country to the farm where his dad and his brothers had grown up and cousins still lived."

"Fat said his dad was in the house, and he was playing in the back pasture with the other kids when he heard his daddy's car start. He said he ran around the house in time to see his daddy's car heading over the hill, dust flying behind his Cadillac. His daddy left him there and never said a word. He never saw his dad again until Fat was twelve and he showed up to move Fat to The Heights."

Silence gripped the group. They all had their daddies. They'd never been taken to some stranger's house, dropped off, and left. They understood Fat's pain. They hated the family that had caused his pain.

Since Fat had never talked about his time before The Heights, they all wished they didn't know now what they didn't know then. "Fat cried when he told me. The first time I've seen him cry," Truck ended.

Truck dried his own eyes. The fellas all wiped their eyes.

Truck picked back up, "I went to his real mama's funeral in North Birmingham a few years ago. Fat came back for it. He was dressed sharply like always. He never cried. He just stood there looking down at the casket. His dad was not there. I don't think he knew many of the people."

Radio and Cool remembered another time when Fat had cried, but they didn't interrupt.

. . .

The light tap on the door interrupted things. It was almost dark. Who could it be?

A young woman walked in. Fat dragged himself up in the bed. He smiled and called to her. "Come here girl and give your brother a hug. Y'all know my sister."

It was Fat's half-sister. The fellas knew her but didn't recognize her. They had only known her as a little girl. She gave Fat a hug and a kiss on the cheek and reached for a chair, but Fat made room for her on the bed. "Sit next to your brother," he implored her. Fat's face broke into the biggest smile. He grabbed her hand.

Fat's sister, Karen, looked more like her mother than the fellas were comfortable with. She smiled back at her brother. She was glad to see him. She had been only seven when he left and she wouldn't know why until years later. "I love you," she leaned in and whispered to Fat. Fat's look told everyone in the room, the trip had been worth it. Another tear rolled out of Fat's other eye.

"I love you," he answered.

The fellas went outside to check out Fat's new Cadillac and to give Fat and his sister some privacy. They could see Fat was touched. He'd hardly known her, and she gave him the sense of family he'd always wanted. He wouldn't turn her hand loose.

Karen would be the only one in his family to visit him.

Later, with the company all gone, the fellas settled in to

conclude their visit with their old friend.

"So, Truck, how them boys of yours?" Fat asked.

Truck laughed. "My boys?"

"Hell yeah, your boys. Who you think I'm talking about?" Fat roared. "You the only one here beside me with boys. Cool done spit out a couple of girls. Radio and Goose still trying to figure it out."

"How old your boys?" Fat wanted to know.

"Fourteen and sixteen," Truck answered. "The oldest one is smelling his own piss. Think he's grown."

"Smelling his own piss." The words hung in the air like a foul odor. Cool's eyes darted to Radio's. Fat dropped his.

. . .

After the fight, with Fat having whipped his two brothers and they had run for home, Truck and Goose had gone to Truck's house to play Bid Whist. Truck's parents let the boys and other neighbor kids use their basement to play cards, listen to music, dance, and generally hang out. It was the neighborhood club for the kids.

Radio and Cool decided to wait on Fat and promised to be there later.

They drifted toward Fat's house. They knew better than to go to the door. They very seldom went to Fat's house. They never went inside. Every one of the other fellas' homes you could visit, but not Fat's. It wasn't his home. He just lived there.

Fat would probably get a whipping, and then everything would be all right. They all got whippings except for Radio. His mom believed in punishment. She would refuse to let him go out and play after school. Compared to the light whippings they got, the fellas would prefer the whippings to punishment because it would be over shortly, and the playing could continue.

Radio and Cool had a wild idea. They decided to listen. It was something they'd done before. When one of them would get a whipping they would listen, and later, while under the streetlight, they would replay the sounds of the whipping and jump around like they were getting whipped as a joke. "Ow, Ow, Ow," they would yell. Everyone would laugh at the one who got whipped.

Radio and Cool slipped into the hedges in front of Fat's porch. They could hear screams. They could hear JuneBug and Randy telling how Fat had beaten them. Michael and Randy's mom was screaming at her husband, Fat's daddy. "I told you. I told you. He's an animal."

"Get out of here, all of you!" Fat's daddy hollered. Radio and Cool knew the whipping was about to come. *Good,* they thought. They knew Fat could handle it and they would be playing cards soon.

The *WHAP, WHAP, WHAP!* started as the belt sliced across Fat's skin. "Get them damn clothes off," the dad commanded. *WHAP! WHAP! WHAP!* The beating picked up. "I told you. I told you," he said.

WHAP! WHAP! WHAP! WHAP! WHAP! WHAP! WHAP! The whipping went on and on.

At first, Radio and Cool laughed, but the beating continued and they could hear Fat start to whimper as the whaps got louder and louder. It was no longer funny.

WHAP! WHAP! WHAP! WHAP!

"You smelling your own piss ain't cha boy!" Fat's daddy hollered. "Well, Goddamn it, I done had enough of it."

WHAP! WHAP! WHAP! WHAP! WHAP! WHAP! WHAP! It continued.

Fat burst out in a loud wailing cry. *WHAP! WHAP! WHAP!*

"Shut your damn mouth!" his dad commanded.

WHAP! WHAP! WHAP!

Fat whimpered.

WHAP, WHAP...! WHAP!

Finally, it was over.

Radio and Cool cowered in the bushes. It was the worst whipping they'd ever heard. It was brutal and savage, with lots of pent up anger behind every lash across Fat's body. Radio tried to hold his tears but couldn't. He let them go in a silent cry. Cool turned his head as his tears fell. They crawled out of the bushes and slowly headed for Truck's.

Fat never knew they were there. They never brought it up to anybody.

. . .

Fat, laughing, energized, and feeling good after his sister's visit, got the courage to make the trip to the bathroom. Tin Man, all 170 pounds of him, helped lift his friend, who outweighed him by a hundred and forty pounds, out of the bed. The fellas all stood up to help, but Fat waved them off.

"Tin Man's got it. Shee-it, that's what I pay him for." Fat and Tin dragged his dulled left side into the restroom. Fat took care of his business while the fellas waited outside.

When Fat emerged again from the bathroom, the biggest grin he could remember in a long time spread across his face, left side included. The fellas were up singing, "The Tracks of My Tears," and mimicking the choreographed dance moves of Smokey Robinson and The Miracles, like they all had done as youngsters.

"We need a lead singer," Goose laughed as they sang the chorus.

> *"So take a good look at my face.*
> *You see my smile looks out of place.*
> *If you look closer it's easy to trace, the tracks of my tears.*
> *Woo-oo, I need you. Need you."*

"Come on Fat, you the man," Radio encouraged. They motioned for Fat to join in and sing the lead.

Fat pushed Tin Man aside and dragged himself into the lead position in the group. He danced along with the steps as best he could with the good side of his body.

He sang.

> *"People say I'm the life of the party 'cause I tell a joke or two.*
> *Although I might be laughing loud and hearty, deep inside I'm blue."*

The fellas joined in the chorus, *"So take a good look at my face..."*

Once again, they were back in The Heights, grinning, dancing, and singing. Fat and the Boys, Smokey Robinson and the Miracles.

About the Author

Thom Gossom, Jr. is an actor and author. His memoir, *Walk-On: My Reluctant Journey to Integration at Auburn University*, is his story as the first African American athlete to graduate from Auburn. Additional works include a critically acclaimed play, *Speak Of Me As I Am*, the blog *As I SEE It*, and contributions to *The Birmingham News* and *The Birmingham Times*.

The *Slice of Life* collection of life stories continues with *Another Slice of Life* and *The Rest of The Pie*.

On television, Gossom starred as Israel, the title character in the Emmy® winning *NYPD Blue* episode "Lost Israel." Other television credits include *Reckless, Drop Dead Diva, Game of Your Life, CSI, Boston Legal, ER,* and *Miss Ever's Boys*. Film credits include *Fight Club* and *Jeepers Creepers 2*.

Gossom and his wife live in Fort Walton Beach, Florida.
Visit www.BestGurl.com or facebook.com/BestGurlinc

Books by Thom Gossom Jr.
Another Slice of Life
The Rest of The Pie
Walk-On

www.ingramcontent.com/pod-product-compliance
Lightning Source LLC
Chambersburg PA
CBHW070631120726
47909CB00004B/1385